The Cost of Loyalty 2

Kweli

Lock Down Publications and Ca$h
Presents

The Cost of Loyalty 2
A Novel by *Kweli*

Kweli

Lock Down Publications
P.O. Box 870494
Mesquite, Tx 75187

Visit our website @
www.lockdownpublications.com

Copyright 2019 The Cost of Loyalty 2

First Edition May 2019
Printed in the United States of America

Lock Down Publications
Like our page on Facebook: Lock Down Publications @
www.facebook.com/lockdownpublications.ldp
Cover design and layout by: **Dynasty Cover Me**
Book interior design by: **Shawn Walker**
Edited by: **Tisha Andrews**

4

Stay Connected with Us!

Text **LOCKDOWN** to 22828 to stay up-to-date with new releases, sneak peaks, contests and more...

Thank you.

Submission Guideline

Submit the first three chapters of your completed manuscript to ldpsubmissions@gmail.com, subject line: Your book's title. The manuscript must be in a .doc file and sent as an attachment. Document should be in Times New Roman, double spaced and in size 12 font. Also, provide your synopsis and full contact information. If sending multiple submissions, they must each be in a separate email.

Have a story but no way to send it electronically? You can still submit to LDP/Ca$h Presents. Send in the first three chapters, written or typed, of your completed manuscript to:

LDP: Submissions Dept
Po Box 870494
Mesquite, Tx 75187

DO NOT send original manuscript. Must be a duplicate.

Provide your synopsis and a cover letter containing your full contact information.

Thanks for considering LDP and Ca$h Presents.

ACKNOWLEDGEMENTS

Shout out to my right hand, B. Itabiyi. What's understood, don't need to be explained. You know what it is, Fam.

My young homie, B.D. Twan, who now back in them Chiraq trenches. Ain't no room for error, G, so move accordingly.

Ca$h, I'll always be grateful to you for givin' me the opportunity to share my mind with the world. An' a special thanx for answering yo' phone every single time I've ever called you.

A shout out to all the real ones from my hometown, Toledo, Ohio. No matter how far I go, I can never forget where I came from. (R.I.P. To Jonathan "Jon-Jon" Booker, and Clifford "Suge" Robinson.)

To my comrades from Cincinnati, Kwabana "Boss" Anderson, Joseph "Joe" Watkins, and R.I.P. to Rico "Smoke" Spencer (Moosewood).

To every King & Queen with exceptional loyalty an' integrity. Whether you sellin' property or pounds of pressure, a double salute!

Kweli

Chapter 1

When Terry Jones got within several feet, J-Bo froze up as his eyes widened in disbelief. After fantasizing about this day for years, he was finally standing face-to-face with his mother's killer.

Terry Jones had a similar reaction. He, too, was unable to believe he was actually staring into the pair of eyes that had been haunting him in his dreams for the past eleven years.

As both men speechlessly stood before each other, they couldn't help but recall the night that had forever changed their lives.

Hurriedly pushing him into a small closet, J-Bo's mother Simone firmly held his face in her hands as she told him to stay put. "I don't care what you hear, do not come out of this closet. You understand me?" Picking up on the urgency in her tone, he quickly nodded. "An' no matter what happens, I want you to always remember that I really did love you. I know it wasn't easy for you, but momma did the best she could."

Hearing footsteps rapidly approaching, Simone kissed his forehead and quietly shut the door. While frantically searching for a means of protection, the bedroom door was booted off its hinges.

The glare in his eyes colder than the paws of a polar bear, Terry Jones stepped inside the room. He was there to crush the head of a snake. "Terry, please," Simone pleaded as she backpedaled toward the side of the room. "It ain't what you think, baby. Somebody broke in an' stole it an' I just didn't know how to tell you."

Her words falling on deaf ears, he withdrew a revolver from the small of his back. "You'll never bite no one else," he coldly stated before he blew her down, then stood over the body and put another through her heart.

As he turned to leave, Terry froze in surprise when he saw a child's face in the partially opened doorway of a closet. Judging him to be at least nine years old, he knew what had to be done. Leveling the gun with the boy's tear-stained face, he made the mistake of looking into his eyes.

While he had committed some monstrous acts in his past, the killing of a defenseless child was a boundary his heart would not allow him to cross. With a blank expression, he lowered the gun and quickly fled the room.

Recovering from his initial shock, J-Bo drew his strap and aimed it at Terry Jones' face. Juan-Juan's friend or not, death was his only option.

His eyes displaying no fear, Terry lifted his chin and stated, "Do what you gotta do."

Before he closed his curtains, there was one thing J-Bo had to know. "Why you do it?"

"Cause she betrayed me," Terry answered in an unremorseful tone.

Involved in everything from armed robberies to Zanny bars, Terry Jones had the game in a vicious chokehold when he crossed paths with Simone. Sly as a fox with exotic features, no kids, and the sexual performance of a porn star, it wasn't long before she had his nose wide open.

Two years into their relationship, Terry was arrested for the shooting of a man who he told authorities had tried to rob him. Although his story was convincing, he was denied bond since he was already on parole for a prior assault. It was then he placed Simone behind the desk of his empire. A costly mistake that would teach him the meaning of misplaced loyalty.

Driven by greed and the firm belief that Terry would get a football number in prison, Simone hopped in his XLR with $487,000 and moved down to Dayton. Craving the companionship and protection of a man, she soon fell into the arms of an older cat named Money-Wise. Shrewd by nature, it was only a matter of time before he put the pieces together.

They came home one morning from a night of partying to discover that Simone's house had been broken into and ransacked. Dashing upstairs to her bedroom, she let out a piercing scream when she saw the dresser tipped over. After crying herself to sleep, she woke up later that day to find Money-Wise missing along with the last bit of money that had been in her purse.

Afraid to continue living there alone, she sold her recently bought appliances and moved back to Toledo where she was soon hit with another blow that brought her to her knees.

Meanwhile, Terry Jones sat inside the county jail boiling with rage. After all he'd done for Simone, she didn't even have the decency to retain him a lawyer. While he blamed himself for giving her the chance to sink her fangs into him, he felt like she had inflicted a wound that only her death could heal. And his hunger for revenge is what would carry him through a ten-year sentence.

"An' I have only one regret," Terry Jones admitted to J-Bo as he held his stare. "That you were there to witness it."

As J-Bo considered his spiel, he was suddenly struck by a reality he would've overlooked had it not been for the situation with Olivia. She had also committed a violation to the point where her actions were punishable by death.

Although it was shrewd, the reality was that the game was governed by certain rules. And regardless of who the player was, family or friend, the rules applied to *everyone.*

Like Olivia, his mother had put down a play so foul that it could not possibly be ignored. To intentionally betray a good man is inexcusable. So, while he didn't necessarily *agree* with what Terry Jones had done, he could now *understand* it.

Because now, after all, they were no different. They had both killed women they once loved on the strength of principles. And as he compared Terry's appearance from back then to the shell of a man now standing before him, he knew there was no sense in killing someone who was already dead.

Lowering his gun, J-Bo broke the awkward silence as he glanced at his watch, saying he had to get back in traffic. "But Juan-Juan wanted you to have this," he added as he tossed him the small duffel bag.

Terry wordlessly caught it without looking inside.

Neither man knowing what else to say, they exchanged a slight nod before backing up and turning to go their separate ways.

As J-Bo went back to his car, he had to smirk at the crazy way life could sometimes play out. Here it was, Juan-Juan had unknowingly been a close friend with his mother's killer all this time which made him wonder how he would've handled the situation had he found out. Because J-Bo knew that if he and Terry Jones had bumped heads just a month ago, it would've been a whole different ball game.

J-Bo was so lost in thought that he didn't peep the ski-masked men soundlessly appearing out of the darkness with MP5 submachine guns.

"TPD! Get on the ground! Get on the ground!"

Red beams crisscrossing over his face and chest, J-Bo's body tensed up in fear as he looked around wild-eyed like a trapped animal. Not only was he boxed in, but he had put the strap back on his waist. He wouldn't get off a single shot if he reached.

"Get on the ground *now!*" one of the faceless men warned as he inched closer with his beam centered between J-Bo's eyes.

How the fuck they get hip to me, he thought to himself as he slowly got down and placed his hands behind his head.

J-Bo was lying face down on the pavement in cuffs when one of the officers rolled him onto his back. Lifting his mask to reveal a smile of satisfaction, Detective Sterling teased, "Remember me, cocksucker?"

While seated in the back of an unmarked cruiser waiting to be transported downtown, J-Bo paid no attention to a red CTS as it slowly drove by. The same car had been at the gas pump behind him when he stopped at the B.P.

Chapter 2

Later That Night

The Pulse was jumping as Yo Gotti stood center stage performing hood anthems off his Cocaine Muzic album. Resembling a live recording of the show, *Gang Land*, the club was crowded with homicidal hooligans who were proudly reppin' their sets. Their already reckless natures boosted by alcohol, a funeral or two was definitely in the making.

In designer outfits with traces of red to represent their Blood affiliation, D-Wub, his lieutenant, Suge, and three of their most active assassins, Ghost, Moo-Moo, and Bhomas held down a section directly in front of the stage. A stick of pressure in one hand and a gold bottle in the other, each man was rocking a wolf-head medallion attached to a yellow-gold Cuban choker. From appearance, the Wolf-Pack was being well-fed.

Louis Vuitton-clothed from the shoulders down, Fat-Cat was posted up on the other side of the stage in enough VVSs to rival those of Yo Gotti's. Standing in the center of a large entourage, he was accompanied by his girl, Kiona, his right-hand, Jinx, and a squad of savages from an official Crip set called Geer-Gang.

While he was not a gang member himself, the pill lord understood the importance of having an army. So, for a percentage of his fortune, he enlisted soldiers who would readily risk their lives in exchange for luxurious lifestyles.

With a sparkler in each hand, a fleet of bartenders drew the crowd's attention as they weaved through the club. For the second time that night, they were headed in Fat-Cat's direction with nearly $10,000 in champagne.

"I might drop an opp' tonight, Cuzz!" Shooter grinned as he dumped a gram of Molly inside his bottle and shook it. Ruggedly handsome with shoulder-length dreads over a dark brown complexion, the nineteen-year-old was suspected by the streets of being responsible for several gang-related murders.

"I done fought the best of 'em an' shot the rest of 'em!" Eli drunkenly chimed in before turning up his bottle. Shooter's childhood friend, Eli, was a mixed pretty-boy who was actually mild-tempered by nature. But like most club nights, the mixture of alcohol and Shooter's presence had him on some Randy Savage type shit.

As two others in their circle, Baby-Herc and Blueface, were spraying champagne into the mouths of models, Jinx leaned near Shooter's ear and nudged him. "Aye, come roll wit' me real quick, Cuzz."

A pocket-rocket tucked in the small of his back, Shooter asked no questions as he followed him through the crowd.

Stopping in front of the women's restroom, Jinx flashed a mischievous smile. "Hold me down, Lock," he said before disappearing inside.

At 6'3" with brushed waves over thick eyebrows and a caramel complexion, twenty-three-year-old Jinx was considered a big homie among the younger generation of Crips. Born in it rather then sworn in it, his family's allegiance to the turf had left him with no choice but to accept the baton at an early age.

Lost in the streets after the death of his father, it was Fat-Cat who had led him to the realization that gang-banging and getting money were like oil and water. They didn't mix. And being broke was the trait of a lame. Now nearly a year after being under Fat-Cat's wing, Jinx had close to $200,000 hid inside his granny's house.

Standing before a large mirror adjusting her makeup, a woman inside the restroom saw Jinx enter and instantly reached for her purse. She may have known who he was, but was taking no chances.

"Chill, ma," he said with a smirk as her hand came out with a can of mace. "This ain't that type of party." He then pulled out a colorful bankroll and laid it on the counter. "I ain't gotta take what I can pay fo'."

Her scent of Light Blue by Dolce & Gabana loitering in the air, Ciara eyed the money as a lion would a wounded gazelle. From selling pussy to setting up licks, which she had done for Juan-Juan and J-Bo, her coin addiction was no mystery to herself or anyone else.

Taking her eyes off what she estimated to be no less than five bands, Ciara made sure they were alone, then stepped within arms distance of Jinx and boldly slid her hand inside his Robin jeans. While she held no discrimination in regards to stature or race, a limp dick man was not only a waste of time

Kweli

but outside her boundaries.

After he easily passed the inspection, she cuffed and stashed the money before putting her number in his phone. "Meet me out at the Hawthorne when the club let out. I'll get a room for the night." Then, with her signature strut that was designed to make her loose cheeks jiggle provocatively, Ciara left the bathroom without looking back.

As Jinx came out behind her and saw the line of women angrily waiting to get inside, he smiled at Shooter with an appreciative nod. "Good lookin', Cuzz."

Ciara was headed toward the bar when she was roughly grabbed by the arm. "Bitch, what the fuck you doin' in the bathroom wit' that crab ass nigga?" Bhomas heatedly demanded as he snatched her close. His government name Thomas, the sneaky-eyed twenty-year-old had the words 'Blood Gang' tattooed on the right side of his face.

Not one for public spectacles, Ciara took a deep breath and hissed through clenched teeth, "Let me go or it's *over* between us!"

Flamed-up in a Balmain hoodie and cherry red Chucks, Bhomas saw the sincerity in her eyes and reluctantly released her. "I'm sayin' though, Blood," he said, raking a hand through his red-tipped dreads in anger and frustration. "You up in here fuckin' wit' the opps an' that shit ain't *bool*."

Her face instantly screwing up, Ciara snapped. "Nigga, you act like you my man. Like you payin' all my bills an' shit. Get yo' weight up, then maybe you can dictate who an' what I do. Until then, keep that shit on mute."

"So fuck that shoppin' spree, huh?" Bhomas shot back with balled fists. "Like I ain't drop eight racks on that shit." He had recently flown her out to Cali' where she blew through his savings on a fashion strip in Beverly Hills.

Fully aware of the younger man's infatuation with her, Ciara had gone against her better judgment, deciding to exploit his weakness. But it was the reoccurring tantrums like these that had her now wondering if his contributions were even worth the hassle.

Moving in close enough so that the nipples of her braless C-cups could brush against him, Ciara spoke into his ear, "Not only are you embarrassin' *yourself*, but you're embarrassin' *me*. So I'll call you later, then you can make this up to me wit' some of that fire ass head." Before he could form a reply, she kissed his cheek and stepped off.

His pride hurt, Bhomas angrily stared at her. *I should kill that hoe.*

"What's brackin', homie?" Ghost inquired as he approached Bhomas with a curious expression. "You look like you ready to get them Chucks dirty." A Blood originally from Cali', Ghost was dark skin with a thin build and green eyes. He was by far one of the deadliest canines in the Wolf-Pack.

Bhomas was on the verge of blowing him off when a treacherous play suddenly popped in his head. Lowering his voice to a secretive whisper, he revealed, "I just found out who kilt Fred, Blood."

While Gotti was backstage taking a break, Blueface became the center of attention when he started Crip walking to a Nipsey Hussle song. A royal blue flag hanging from the left side of his back pocket, he mirrored the movements of Dub-C while fluidly throwing up a series of gang signs. The Crips going crazy, he ended the dance by removing his flag and dabbing imaginary sweat from his forehead.

After performing his final song of the night, Yo-Gotti was expressing his love and gratitude for the city when the Wolf-Pack put down a stunt that would be spoken of for days. Climbing onto the stage, D-Wub took off his Versace shirt to reveal a money belt that was fastened around his waist. On cue, Suge magically produced a small money counter. A suspenseful silence fell over the club as D-Wub began feeding the bills into the machine.

Beep!

Sending the club into an instant frenzy, he and his wolves grabbed handfuls of the money and made it rain. Then, to ensure that his statement was made, D-Wub tossed the counter to a known thot and watched her eyes widen in surprise.

The Wolf-Pack had just donated $20,000.

Leaving The Pulse, the Wolf-Pack was all business as they marched militant-like towards matching Vettes. Black-on-black with red calipers and limo tint, they fingered the remote-start buttons and simultaneously awakened the supercharged engines. This being one of D-Wub's survival tactics, they would swerve through traffic until there was no way to determine who was in which car.

Meanwhile, Fat-Cat and his men were seven cars deep as they slowly exited the crowded parking lot. A ready-to-fire Drako lying on the passenger seat, Shooter led the way in his powder-blue '442' skating on gold 30's. With Blueface bringing up the rear in a '14 Camaro, Fat-Cat and Kiona were stationed in the middle comfortably settled in the spacious cabin of an S550. So there was no question in regards to ownership, he had personal plates on the car that read, 'FAT-CAT'S'.

As YFN Lucci quietly rapping inside the cream Mercedes, Fat-Cat was reclining in the passenger seat with a de-cocked semi while Kiona handled the heated wheel. Several blocks from the club, she abruptly slid out of the seven car motorcade and disappeared down a side street.

While Shooter and the others were headed to a B.P., which half the city would cram into, they were going home to prepare for an early-morning flight. At Kiona's insistence, her and Fat-Cat would celebrate their one-year anniversary in Montego Bay, Jamaica.

As they were approaching the entrance ramp to the E-Way, an SRT Dodge Ram on 6's suddenly sped alongside them, causing Fat-Cat's hand to instinctively tighten on his firearm. His man Jinx, who had been trailing the sedan since leaving the club, lowered his window far enough to salute, then punched the gas and rumbled off into the night.

Although Fat-Cat treated Jinx as he would a brother, there were certain restrictions on their friendship. And knowing where he laid his head was one. He was simply applying the wisdom in Boosie's song, "Trust Nobody".

***

After refusing to give a statement, J-Bo was taken to a secluded area of the police station where several steroid-injecting officers tried to *force* a confession out of him. Once they realized the only thing on him that could be broken were his bones, he was thrown into a police car and hauled over to the county jail.

Booked on a slew of felonious charges, he used his one phone call on Wittenburg who answered in a groggy voice, promising he would be to see him first thing in the morning.

Due to the nature of his charges, J-Bo was placed in 6-West, a high-security unit on the sixth floor that was directly behind the C.O.'s control booth. Designed to cause depression, it was a four-man tank with one phone, one TV, one shower, and four windowless cells.

Standing in the center of the room looking around in disbelief, J-Bo slowly shook his head as the reality of his situation fully sunk in. *I'm really locked the fuck up.* Then another thought even more disturbing appeared. *An' I might not ever make it out this bitch.*

Chapter 3

Low-key in a Nissan Altima, Ciara wheeled into the Hawthorne's parking lot and double-parked by the front entry. Leaving the car running, she ran inside to pay the $200 nightly fee, then emerged minutes later with the keycard to a two-level suite.

Jinx witnessed all this from behind the tinted windows of his Dodge Ram. When Ciara's tail lights disappeared around the circular drive that led to the rooms, he put the truck in drive and eased out from between two S.U.Vs.

Parked in front of the room with her car door pushed open, Ciara was reaching for a bag off the passenger seat when a car that swooped in right next to her startled her.

''I should've known," she said with a smirk as Jinx unfolded himself from the truck and came around to her side of the car.

"It's a heartless world," he commented after a brief scan of the Nissan's interior.

Inside the room, Ciara was headed upstairs to change when Jinx called out with a solemn expression, "Aye, let me see yo' phone."

Ciara turned to give him a look of disbelief, to which he wisely replied, "Only *you* know what yo' intentions are."

When coming out of the bathroom ten minutes later in a lace thong, matching bra, and four-inch stilettos, Ciara was caught off guard by what she saw in the center of the room. Standing buck naked, besides his jewelry and blue Jordans, Jinx wore a single-strap shoulder holster with a 17-round glock in it. Under the pit of his left arm, it was positioned to where it would not interfere with his performance.

Ignoring her expression as he crossed the room, he stepped behind her and took a moment to study the fatness of her stretch-marked ass. "So, this what got these niggas out here having sucka attacks," he joked as he smacked the loose cheeks, fascinated by how long they seemed to jiggle.

Ciara took a step forward and started bouncing on the heels of her feet.

Clap! Clap! Clap! Clap! Clap! Clap!

Instantly bricking up, Jinx led her over to the king size bed where he removed all but her heels and pushed her into a seated position. "I gotta an extra nickel if you can make me nut in less than five minutes."

The bonus being music to her ears, she grabbed his joint in one hand, balls in the other, and performed whorish tricks reserved for her future husband.

With his hands on his hips, Jinx looked to his left and flashed a boss-like grin. An iPhone 6 peeking from his coat pocket, the five bands had simply been an investment. Unbeknownst to Ciara, she was starring in a movie he would title, *Ratchet Hoez Exposed.*

The VVSs dancing in the hockey puck on his wrist, Jinx held it eye level for several seconds, then grabbed her head. "Time up, ma."

Her face a wet mess, she stared up at him in defeat as a thick string of saliva clung from her lips to his tip.

This mu'fucka goin' viral! He laughed to himself while strapping up.

Hovering over her with one of his calloused hands gripping the headboard, he gave her time for size adjustment, then began to forcefully dig into her from multiple angles. Fully charged off Molly and Percs, he intended to make her tap.

Determined not to scream as her eyes rolled to back of her head, Ciara could feel herself losing control after every precision-driven stroke. Finding spots only a few had ever found, he was breaking through the business-minded mentality she usually held when it came to such encounters.

"Let me ride it, Jinx!" she pleaded as he showed no signs of exhaustion.

Recognizing her request as a sign of fear, he drugged her quivering body to the bed's edge and forced both legs over her head. Then, with a hunch in his back and unlimited access to her guts, he planted both feet on the floor and made her scream as if he was stabbing her with a knife instead of his dick.

"Jinx!"

"Tap, bitch!"

A car alarm suddenly went off outside. When the small pad attached to his car key began to beep, he quickly pulled out and withdrew the glock. Going over to his clothes, he looked at the small screen and saw that someone had touched his driver side door.

He instantly turned the gun on Ciara. "Bitch, you dying *first*."

"It's Bhomas!" she blurted out. She would not

allow his jealousy to be cause of her death. "He saw us come out the bathroom at the club an' felt some type of way. I fucked him once an' now the nigga think I'm his."

"So how the fuck he know where we at?"

"I don't know," Ciara answered as she racked her brain for a logical explanation. "He must've followed me."

Recalling what he saw at the club, he told her to get dressed and began reaching for his own clothes. T.T.G. at heart, he refused to act in a cowardly manner and barricade himself inside the room. Ending the recording, he texted Shooter his location, then went straight into combat-mode

***

At B.P.

"Smash these niggas, Cuzz!" Eli loudly encouraged Shooter as he was peeling off his shirt. After a heated exchange with a rival from the north side named Bone, Shooter had challenged him and his homie to a two-on-one fist fight.

"Cuzz, you know you trippin', right?" Blueface told Shooter as he stepped in front of him.

"How so?" he questioned defiantly.

"I'm sayin', what you expect me to do? Just stand around an' watch these niggas jump you?" lowering his tone, he suggested. "Let's just catch these niggas later an' put 'em down. 'Cause that's what it's gon' lead to anyway."

His skin the color of Akon's, Blueface stood

5'7" with the build of an action figure. Recently released from an eighteen-month bid in the Department of Youth Services AKA D.Y.S., he was extremely vicious, while at the same time, a critical thinker.

Shooter kissed both sets of his permanently bruised knuckles and grinned. "These bitches gotta mean bite, Cuzz."

"On *the north* y'all better punish this lil' nigga!" an older Blood named Brazy threatened Bone and Quincy as they were bent down tying up their scuffers. "An' whatever they wanna do after that," he said as he thumbed back the hammer on a semi. "We wit' that, too."

The crowd was shoulder-to-shoulder as the three gladiators entered the invisible octagon. Bills in hand, a young boy standing on the hood of his candy-painted drop' yelled out, "I got five hunid on the Crip nigga!"

He instantly ignited a series of bets all over the parking lot, the highest being for $1,200.

His fight game superb, Shooter quickly identified the weaker opponent. He faked as if going straight at Bone, then pivoted toward Quincy and broke his jaw with a leaping left hook.

The crowd went bananas.

An amateur boxer at the Bull Pen, Bone was unfazed by his fallen comrade. As he and Shooter went to head up, he feigned a jab, then fired a crispy overhand that caught him over his right brow. Easily slipping Shooter's counter punches, he decided to toy with his food as he danced out of reach.

Blood trickling over his eye, Shooter realized he would have to turn this into a brawl. So, he purposely ran in on some reckless shit and ate several jabs as he went low and latched on to Bone's jeans. Then, snatching him up off the ground, he slammed him into a pearl-white Denali with thirty-day tags.

"Get the fuck off my shit!" the owner spazzed as he attempted to intervene.

"Watch out, Blood," Brazy warned with the strap held down at his side. "I got twelve hunid on this shit."

Coming from both ways, a flock of police cars suddenly sped up to the gas station. The parking lot too crowded for them to enter, they were lined up in the street with their lights silently flashing.

"Everyone out!" a sergeant ordered over his bullhorn.

The bets instantly forgotten, the crowd scattered, praying they weren't blooped as they drove out.

Shooter hopped up in his oldie, used his shirt as a face cloth, then laid the Drako on his lap before pulling off. Regardless of the charge, prison was a school he would never willingly attend.

A block away, he was reaching for his Pioneer remote when he saw the green light on his phone, alerting him of a missed text. Immediately after reading the short message, he made a U-turn in traffic and called the cavalry.

***

Using Ciara as a shield, Jinx cautiously exited the hotel room. The glock extended over her shoulder, he swept it back and forth as he scanned the parking lot for any movement.

Fop! Fop! Fop! Fop! Fop!

Five rapid shots rang out as Ghost rolled from under an F150.

Reacting without hesitation, Jinx pushed Ciara one way and moved the other, while busting in the enemy's direction.

Boc! Boc! Boc! Boc! Boc! Boc! Boc!

Doom! Doom! Doom! Dom! Doom! Doom!

The target of a second gunman, Jinx got low and ran in between cars. Shards of glass rained down as Bhomas chased after him dumping.

Doom! Doom! Doom! Doom! Doom!

Fueled by emotion, Bhomas emptied his whole thirty before realizing his mistake.

Boc! Boc! Boc! Boc! Boc! Boc!

Now it was Bhomas who was forced to retreat as Jinx lifted his arm over a car and returned fire.

Jinx was reaching for another clip when he was frozen by the sudden appearance of a person's shadow. His footsteps as quiet as a kitten's, Ghost had crept up on him. Wearing an evil sneer, he said, "Good night, Blood." Then pursed his lips and squeezed.

Click!

Click-click-click!

Ghost smirked. "You won't be this lucky next time," he promised as he backed away before turning to run.

Exhaling in relief, Jinx slapped the clip in, then

hurried around to the Ram only to find the tires on the driver side flattened. Police sirens growing louder by the second, he was on the verge of panicking when the game god sent one of its angels.

"Jump in the backseat!" Ciara barked as she sped up and popped the locks.

Cop cars were racing into the Hawthorne just as she was exiting.

Forcing herself to maintain the speed limit as she kept her eyes glued to the rearview, she assured Jinx several minutes later. "I think we good."

Curled up on the backseat with the glock still in hand, he pulled out his phone and dialed Shooter.

Chapter 4

Four deep in a navy blue Charger, Scat Pack edition, Shooter and the others were already parked at the BW3s when Ciara and Jinx drove up. A kush stick in rotation, you could here a low thump of bass as Bobby Shmurda encouraged their murderous intentions.

When the Scat-Pack's interior was illuminated as Blueface went to jump in the backseat, Jinx told Ciara not to leave before hopping out. Going to the back door on the driver side, he opened it and ordered Baby-Herc out of the car.

He shook his head. "Naw, Cuzz. I'm rollin', too."

"Get the fuck out the car, Anthony!" Jinx barked, addressing him by his government to let him know he was dead-ass.

On a full scholarship at U.T. AKA the University of Toledo, Baby-Herc was a star running back who currently led the MAC division in rushing yards. Minus a serious injury or criminal charges, his spot in the N.F.L. was solidified.

At 5'10" and an explosive 225 pounds of muscle, he was being compared to Ohio State's Ezekial Elliott. But it was his false sense of loyalty to the hood that could lead to his downfall.

Before ushering Baby-Herc into the car with Ciara, Jinx quietly schooled him while they were out of earshot. "Cuzz, you actually gotta chance to do somethin' big wit' yo' life.

So, don't fuck that up by thinkin' you owe somethin' to me or anybody else. If you really wanna support the homies, then take yo' ass to the league an' get them M's, nigga."

Jinx flashed a humorous smile and added, "Cause I'ma need you to start repayin' me some of this money I been spendin' on yo' big grown ass."

Nodding his head in understanding, Baby-Herc smiled as he slid down into the car. "A'ight, I got you, big homie."

It was true. Since joining Fat-Cat's team, Jinx ensured that Baby-Herc wanted for nothing. He had copped him a low-mileage Mustang, took him to the mall frequently, and gave him $500 every Friday. His only requirement was that he stay in school and away from the streets.

"Make sho' my lil' nigga get home safe," Jinx advised Ciara as he leaned down into the car.

"He far from a lil' nigga," she replied, eyeing Baby-Herc's massive thighs. "But don't worry, I got 'im."

After watching the Nissan drive out of the parking lot, Jinx hopped in the passenger seat of the Skat-Pack and snapped. "Don't you niggas *ever* bring Baby-Herc around no shit like this! It's bad enough we brought 'im to the club. Fuck was you niggas thinkin'?"

As Shooter gunned the Hemi down Dorr Street like he was a licensed driver, he called for the blunt, then turned Bobby back up and looked forward to putting another one under his belt.

***

Using the two-way to give Eli their location, he

sped up a minute later with the headlights off. As they hopped back inside the car, Shooter leaned up from the backseat and announced what he had in mind.

"Nigga, you *foolin*!" Blueface said as he turned to face him. "We ain't got time for that shit!"

Shooter ignored him and tapped the side of Eli's seat. "Shoot back over there, Cuzz."

"This nigga 'bout to have us on death row," Blueface mumbled to himself, slowly shaking his head.

Pulling into an alley that ran behind Mulberry, Shooter and Blueface grabbed two items from the trunk, then hurried back to the crime scene. The still warm bodies lying in pools of blood, they hastily worked together in carrying out Shooter's wishes.

With the dead men's D.N.A. all over their clothes, Shooter took a moment to admire his work before he caught up with Blueface and they ran back to the car.

Slouched in the backseat as the Scat-Pack zipped down the alley, Shooter fired up a Newport and deeply inhaled. Inwardly excited, he could picture the news coverage as reporters from every station alerted the city of the heinous crime committed in the early morning hours.

"Two local teens were found shot to death in the 1200 block of Mulberry. Placed side-by-side in the middle of the street, their remains were stuffed inside of black body bags..."

Unlike any gang war previously fought in the city, they had just set the tone in what would become a month long blood bath.

Kweli

Chapter 5

At 6 a.m., the county's cell doors were popped for breakfast. Curious to see who the three others inside the tank were, J-Bo slid his door back and stepped out.

A heavily tatted biker with long hair and a beard was watching TV from an angle where he could also see whoever came out of their room. His hard eyes studied J-Bo for a brief second, then rolled back toward the screen.

Two shirtless gladiators from the west side, Young-Loc and Tooly, then popped out of the middle cells, openly sizing J-Bo up.

"Where you from, Cuzz?" Young-Loc asked in a confrontational manner.

"I grew up on the South," J-Bo answered with direct eye contact. "But I don't bang. I get *money.*"

The tension was put on hold as a trustee and two deputies entered the tank with their breakfast trays. "Steak an' eggs," the old convict joked as he sat the food on a small round table with four attached seats.

"Cell one has a lawyer visit!" a female C.O. yelled from inside the control booth.

"Just bang on the glass when you done eating," one of the deputies told J-Bo as they were leaving.

He waved his hand at the trays dismissively. "I'on wont that shit."

J-Bo was led to a room designated for non-contact visits. Eyeing Wittenburg through the plexi glass with a questioning look, he took a seat on the metal stool and picked the receiver up.

"Don't worry about it, kid," Wittenburg assured

him. "I'll have it taken care of by our next visit."

J-Bo nodded, knowing his capabilities were endless. Then, recalling the brief spiel he had rehearsed in his cell, he pled his case. "Look, 'Berg, I don't know if I can beat this shit or not. But I do know I'm in for a serious fight. An' wit' that in mind, I can't think of a better coach to have in my corner than you." Lifting his eyebrows for emphasis, he added, "I need you, 'Burg."

Wittenburg replied in a business-like manner, "While I cannot yet provide you with any guarantees as to what your outcome will be, I am more than willing to assist you in what we can literally call, 'A fight for your life'. Because I assure you, Jovante, that is exactly what they want."

J-Bo sighed in relief. "Good lookin', 'Burg. I swear you don't know how much I appreciate this. 'Cause if you can pull this off, I'll be indebted to you *forever*."

"Speaking of which, you know they'll have your charges trumped up to the max when the indictment comes down. But since this is not our first rodeo, I'll cut you some slack. So if you could just have someone bring me $50,000 in cash, check, or money order, then that'll get the ball to rolling. And we can discuss the remaining fee at a later date."

This was the moment J-Bo had been regretting. "I'on got it right now, 'Burg."

"Well, how much of it do you have?"

J-Bo looked down and mumbled, "Everything I had was in the trunk of that car."

A moment of silence lingered in the air before Wittenburg sat back and glanced at his timepiece.

"Clearly you can understand that I am not in a position to take on a case of this magnitude pro bono. I mean, the time, energy, and resources would be staggering. But what I can do is put in a word to the Public Defender's office and recommend that you be assigned their top lawyers."

"Come on, 'Burg. You know they can't do nothin' wit' no shit like this. They'll get me booked before the trial even start."

"I'm not trying to be difficult, Mr. Bowden. But I run a law firm, not a charity foundation."

Controlled by his emotions, J-Bo blurted out, "But I thought we was cool. You actin' like I can't get out an' get you the money."

Slowly shaking his head, Wittenburg smiled in a way that was meant to express his sadness at J-Bo's perception of their relationship. "You have a lot to learn, Mr. Bowden. This has always been business and nothing more. In each of our prior dealings, was there not a mutual exchange? You must come to the understanding that in life, favors are for friends and business is business."

Without giving J-Bo a chance to reply, Wittenburg rose from his seat and knocked on the door. When a deputy unlocked it, he glanced over his shoulder before stepping out. "Good luck."

From the visiting room, J-Bo was taken down to the basement and placed in a single-man bullpen. As he sat on the wooden bench waiting to appear for arraignment, he inwardly scolded himself for being so naive. Though he hated to admit it, every word Wittenburg spoke was true. He had rocked his own self to sleep and the lawyer had simply been a wake-up call.

While staring at one of the graffiti-covered walls, he cracked a slight grin as he suddenly understood the reason behind the non-contact visit. *Ol' Wittenburg think he got all the sense.*

Surrounded by four deputies as he was being led to the courtroom, J-Bo kept his head tucked as cameramen snapped dozens of pictures and reporters fired off just as many questions.

"Is it true that the bombing of the Columbus Police Station was merely a diversion for the elaborate bank robbery?"

"Did you really murder two of your accomplices for sexually assaulting a female employee?

Due to all the commotion, everyone was taken by surprise when a man appeared out of nowhere and attacked J-Bo, managing to clamp his hands around his neck.

"Where is she?" he cried out, his voice booming throughout the hallways.

As two deputies pried his fingers apart and physically restrained him, Olivia's father, Dr. Patterson, stared at J-Bo with a tortured expression. "Please tell me where my daughter is. If you ever loved her, then at least let me give her a decent burial."

After Dr. Patterson filed a missing persons report, detectives had questioned J-Bo in regards to Olivia's disappearance. But without any leads or a confession, they informed Dr. Patterson that there was nothing they could do.

The cameras were going berserk as J-Bo returned his stare and replied, "I can't help you."

The Cost of Loyalty 2

During his brief appearance inside the courtroom, J-Bo pled not guilty to all charges, then was denied bond on the basis he'd soon be released into the custody of Franklin County where he would be tried on all counts.

On the elevator ride back up to the sixth floor, his thoughts were centered on going to his room and lying down. But as he saw Young-Loc and Tooly eyeing him through the glass in anticipation, he knew sleep was out of the question.

This shit don't end, he thought tiredly to himself as he rolled his neck and cracked his knuckles.

When he stepped inside the tank prepared to swing, Young-Loc screwed his face up and barked, "Nigga, why you ain't tell us you J-Bo?"

Feeling and instant relief, he smiled. "Cause you never asked."

For the next hour, J-Bo listened in amusement as the two eighteen-year-olds excitedly recited some of he and Juan-Juan's felonious exploits; legendary tales they had picked up from the streets.

"An' from what they say, Cuzz," Tooly said with genuine admiration in his eyes. "The homie Juan-Juan had *mass* birthdays under his belt."

Ready to put some pressure on his rack, J-Bo was on the verge of saying he was about to lay it down when they invited him into their room and urged him to take whatever he needed. No longer having any outside support, he was forced to put his pride aside and humbly accept the donations.

Kweli

Chapter 6

Seated on a leather couch inside Ciara's condo, her and her best friend Neicy were discussing last night's events when a pajama wearing little girl bolted into the room.

"Momma, momma!" Savannah sang as she flew into Ciara's arms.

Her weary eyes instantly lit up. "Hi, baby!"

"Me an' auntie Neicy watched Sponge Bob last night. An' him an' Mr. Crab gave Sandy a party."

"Oh really?" Ciara said as she shot Neicy an appreciative glance. "So is momma's angel tryna say she wants a party, too?"

Her expression adorable, Savannah answered, "Wellll, if you insist."

As both women shared a laugh, Ciara's phone started vibrating on the coffee table.

It was Bhomas.

"Go to your room, Savannah. I'll be there in a minute."

"Ok, momma," she obediently replied before running off. "Bye, Auntie Neicy!"

"Bye, baby," She said over her shoulder, then turned back and hissed at Ciara, "Girl, *fuck* that bitch ass nigga. He almost got you killed. Text his lame ass back an' tell him it's a wrap!"

Collecting her thoughts, Ciara wordlessly lit a Newport king and blew smoke toward the ceiling. After a number of mind-soothing pulls, she stubbed it out and began to explain.

"I'm dealin' wit' a very emotional ass nigga, Neicy. I fucked up. But for the sake of me an' my daughter, I can't just cut 'im off like that. I'ma have to rock his ass to sleep until we make our move."

Best friends since grade school, her and Neicy had plans of migrating to a bigger city where they would open up a 24-hour daycare center.

"We can leave *now*, Ciara," Neicy said as reached over and grabbed her hand. "You know I got that raise last year. I've been pullin' doubles out the ass, an' I ain't even gotta tell you what's mine is yours." A four-year employee at Macy's, Neicy had a decent-sized savings account and was eager to make the transition.

"I know, girl," Ciara said and smiled, squeezing her hand. "But just gimme another month to finish runnin' this check up. Then we outta here, I promise."

As Ciara was walking Neicy to the front door, she reached inside her bra and came out with three hundred dollar bills.

Neicy looked down at her hand and frowned. "I know you ain't tryna pay me for watchin' my own goddaughter." Unable to have any children of her own, she loved Savannah as if she herself had carried her for nine months.

"Of course not," Ciara said as she pressed the money into her mitt. "But I know how hard you work for what you got. So just take it."

After waving Neicy goodbye, Ciara closed the door and went to go play with Savannah.

Besides Neicy, only few people knew where Ciara lived or even the fact that she had a six-year-old daughter. Craftiness in her blood, she had carefully created a barrier between her personal life and illicit affairs. But she was forgetful of one thing, karma was inescapable.

***

In the heart of the North side, Eli pulled the Scat-Pack up to the corner of Chestnut and Page. With extendos concealed beneath their red hoodies, Shooter and Blueface hopped out and took off on foot.

Casually bending the corner, Eli drove two blocks down and parked on a darkened side street. A Nascar driver behind the wheel, he would wait in the car with a two-way while the two poachers went hunting.

In spite of his protests toward being dropped off, it was Blueface who convinced Jinx to play the sideline during this scrimmage. "We can't afford for you to get caught up, Cuzz. So let the lil' homies earn they stars an' bars."

As Blueface and Shooter were mobbing up Mulberry, they spotted two potential opps coming out of a beige house across the street. Their faces partially hidden by the red hoodies, they moved their trigger hands near the bottom of their sweaters and began closing in.

Behind the attempt on Jinx's life, immediate retaliation was *mandatory*. So, until Ghost and Bhomas could be tracked down, a straggler or two would be sufficient.

Loudly debating over who was a better player between Le'Bron and Durant, the two north siders went mute as they saw Blueface and Shooter crossing the street.

"What's poppin', Blood?" Shooter greeted as he threw up the 'B' with his left hand, drawing their attention away from his other.

"What's brackin', homie?" the taller one spoke up, feeling instant relief.

"Naw, nigga," Blueface corrected him as he came out with a blue-steel .45 "It's what's *craccin'*!"

Realizing it was an ambush, the taller one cut out without hesitation.

Blueface extended his arm, then closed one eye and squeezed.

Boom! Boom! Boom! Boom! Boom!

Each shot finding its mark, the young track star cried out before tumbling to the ground and lying deathly still. Erasing all chances of survival, Blueface jogged down on him and put one in the back of his head.

Tears unashamedly pouring down his face, Shooter's man stood before him pleading. "I swear to God I don't bang, my nigga. I play ball for Woodward."

A senior in high school, Larry "LJ" Johnson was indeed the team's point guard. Nothing more than an inactive affiliate of the Bloods, he just so happened to be in the wrong place at the wrong time.

Shooter offered him a way out. "Get down an' kiss one of my shoes, Cuzz, or I'ma treat you like a opp'."

Fearfully watching Shooter as he slowly bent down, LJ leaned in to kiss one of his navy blue Air-

Maxes when Shooter fired a head shot at point blank range.

Boc!

"You a cold-blooded ass nigga," Blueface said, laughing as they fled in between two houses.

Not far from Ciara's condo, D-Wub and Bella were parked down the street from an Arab-owned convenience store called One-Stop-Shop. Well-trained, Bella patiently sat on the passenger seat with her focus in the same direction as her master's.

During their nine day stakeout, D-Wub had witnessed several of the city's heaviest heroin suppliers enter the store and minutes later, exit with two bags allegedly filled with groceries.

Like clockwork, it was a few minutes after 10 a.m. when the owner, Abdullah, came out of the store carrying a small duffel bag. Flanked by two Chaldean mercenaries, he laid the bag on the back seat of a late model Audi A8, then pulled off with the two giants trailing in a black Excursion.

Tracking Abdullah through a small device he had placed under the A8 days ago, D-Wub waited a full minute before easing into traffic. This was a power-move where timing and execution was everything.

While driving back toward the inner city, he reached over and scratched behind Bella's clipped ears. "You love me, girl?"

As if understanding his question, she looked at him and answered with a soundless bark.

Sometimes D-Wub wondered if Bella was in any way affected by the removal of her vocal chords. If she knew the volume of her bark was different than the ordinary dog's bark. While his initial intention had only been to create a canine that was vicious and silent, his love for Bella had grown indescribably. Able to read his moods, she knew when to be distant, dangerous or like at the present moment, affectionate.

***

Outside a large hangar, a gleaming white G4 Gulfstream450 was being impregnated with over 30,000 pounds of jet fuel. Scheduled for takeoff in under an hour, two pilots were already settled inside the European-styled cockpit, where data and digital images were displayed on 14-inch LCD touch screens.

As a flight attendant from the private jet company was checking his watch, a money-green Ducati came roaring down the tarmac. In third gear, the driver popped the clutch, rolled the throttle, then daringly raised the bike up. He let it down seconds later and began tapping the brake until he came to a stop several feet in front of an attendant.

Hopping off the back in a leather-racing jacket, Kiona took off her helmet and handed it to a concierge.

He eyed it with a puzzled expression. "No luggage, Ms. Mitchell?"

"She good," Fat-Cat spoke up as he replaced his helmet with a pair of Tom Ford aviators. "We'll get everything when we land."

Posing for a number of flicks, many which would be sent behind the fence, Fat-Cat was doing what most hood niggas with money rarely did; enjoy it.

Stepping onto the plane, Fat-Cat asked to meet the pilots before takeoff. "I just wanna lay eyes on the men responsible for my life."

Both pilots captain-qualified, the eldest assured him, "I can understand your concerns, sir, but please know that our safety standards surpass that of the FAA."

Despite being dizzy with excitement, Kiona maintained a diva-like demeanor as she took in the flawlessly furnished cabinetry. While this was her first private jet experience, her composure suggested otherwise.

As the G4 accelerated down the runway, Fat-Cat shot a thirty-second video on J-Pay for his comrades in state prison. His eyes obscured behind the photo-chromic lenses, he looked into the camera and boasted, "Just me an' wifey on a thirteen-seat G4, you hear me? Flyin' straight to Jamaica, no layovers. What's the price? Thirty large? But boy you know that's chicken feed. An' make sho' you check ya books. I just put a band on that bitch!"

The recording ended with him bringing flame up to a stick of Cali' Kush.

Kweli

Chapter 7

Periodically checking his rearview as he coasted through the darkened streets of an upscale neighborhood, Abdullah cautiously circled his block before parking in front of a luxurious four-bedroom. Grabbing a leather satchel off the back seat, he was exiting the car when he noticed a bearded man in a fedora walking up the street. He would've been alarmed by his timing had he not held a walking stick while being guided by a Golden Retriever.

As Abdullah was headed up the pathway leading to his front door, the blind man suddenly tripped over an untied shoelace and went down hard. His glasses going one way and walking stick another, he was on his hands and knees mumbling in panic as he felt around in all the wrong places.

"Here you go, sir," Abdullah said as he held out the glasses.

"Leave me alone!" the blind man cried as he cowered in fear. "I don't have any money."

"Sir, my name is Abdullah and my home is right here," he said unconsciously, pointing toward his house. "I am not here to hurt you."

Helping the blind man to his feet, Abdullah stiffened when he saw that he was palming a silenced .25 semi'.

"Breathe wrong an' it'll be the last breath you take," D-Wub promised as he held the gun waist-level.

"You have no idea of what you're getting yourself into," Abdullah calmly warned. "So, for your own benefit, I encourage you to walk away."

D-Wub smirked in sarcasm. "Help the bear."

After entering Abdullah's house and advising him to type in the right alarm code, D-Wub made him lie face down and secured his wrists and ankles with zip ties. Then, rolling him over, he urged, "Please don't make me look for it."

"You are sadly mistaken if you think I'm foolish enough to keep anything inside my home. There's $156,000 in the bag. I promise you, that's all you'll get from here."

Aside from the picture less and barely furnished rooms, D-Wub knew from his nine-day surveillance that he was standing in Abdullah's stash house. Done talking, he slapped a strip of duct tape over his mouth, then went through the house and opened the door to every room.

Going back outside, D-Wub walked down the street to a white Ford Econoline van and exchanged the Golden Retriever for a toolbox and his beloved Land Shark. He had come thoroughly prepared.

When he reentered the house with Bella trotting alongside him, Abdullah forgot to breathe as he and the massive-headed beast locked eyes. He knew he was staring at a people-biter.

"Last chance," D-Wub warned as he snapped her leash.

His eyes bulging in terror, Abdullah shook his head back and forth while groaning through the tape.

"A man can regain his money but not his life," D-Wub reasoned as he sat the toolbox on the floor and popped the clamps. When he pulled out a big green apple and held it up, Bella instantly went into a seated position while eagerly staring up at him. Green apples were her favorite. And while he couldn't figure out how, she could tell the difference between a green one and a red one.

Swapping the apple for a baggie of heroin, he placed it by her nose until she caught the scent, then ordered, "*Seek!*"

A game they frequently played, Bella went straight into hunt-mode as she executed a thorough sniff of the living room before moving on to other parts of the house.

Fifteen minutes later, with D-Wub's confidence in her beginning to weaken, Bella came back into the living room and barked twice; a signal she'd found something.

He knocked Abdullah unconscious before following her upstairs to an exercise room where she sat next to a state of the art treadmill.

Going inside his box, D-Wub found the tool he needed and began to dismember the machine. With his heart racing in suspense as he unscrewed the bottom half, he popped off the plastic cover and experienced a feeling so euphoric that goosebumps appeared all over his arms. This being a hood niggas' dream, he was face-to-face with vacuum-sealed bricks of heroin.

Her role completed, Bella came and sat before him with her eyes glued to the pocket that held her green apple.

"Woman, you somethin' else," D-Wub smirked as he removed the apple, then split it in half and fed it to her.

After quickly exchanging the tools inside his

box for the fourteen slabs of China White, D-Wub went back downstairs to find that Abdullah had awakened. He held the box up teasingly and joked, "Finders keepers." Then, placing it on the table, he stood over Abdullah and cracked his knuckles. "Now let's get down to business, shall we?"

Bella cocked her head to the side when D-Wub rolled him over and straddled his back. "I ain't never did this before," he admitted to the whimpering man as he gripped his head in one hand and chin in the other. "So, it might hurt a lil' bit."

Abdullah released a muffled scream as D-Wub brutally jerked his head to the side in an attempt to break his neck.

"Told you this my first time," D-Wub said as he laughed, then jerked again.

Still alive, Abdullah passed out from the pain.

This shit can't be that hard, D-Wub said to himself as he reapplied his grip, took a deep breath, then jerked with all his might.

Crack!

He checked Abdullah's pulse to be sure, then looked at Bella in triumph. "I break *necks!*"

She barked once in approval.

Removing the sunglasses and phony beard as they drove off in the van, D-Wub laughed out loud while reaching for his pack of squallies. At the age of twenty-three, he was now officially a multimillionaire.

***

Safe Haven's Nursing Home

"I'm here to see Ms. Gloria Wubbins."

"And you are?"

"De'Angelo Wubbins, her grandson."

Recently hired, the receptionist's fingers danced over the keyboard before requesting his identification.

D-Wub let out an irritated sigh as he began to search for something he knew he didn't have.

"De'Angelo?"

He turned to see that it was Phyllis, a caregiver who had been with Safe Haven for years.

"Hey, Ms. Cunningham."

"Hi, sweetie. You here to see Ms. Gloria?"

"This gentleman doesn't have an I.D., Phyllis," the receptionist cut in. "An' you know policy states—"

"Child, hush. I know policy. But I also know how much Ms. Gloria gon' love to see her grandbaby." She waved D-Wub forward. "C'mon now, let's get you back there."

Ms. Gloria was seated in front of the window when D-Wub entered the room. "Phyllis?" she called out without turning around.

"No, Nana. It's me."

"My baby!" she joyfully exclaimed as she rose from the chair and hurriedly felt her way over to him. Diagnosed with glaucoma disease, Ms. Gloria had been declared legally blind nearly ten years ago.

"What have you done to your hair, De'?" She asked in humor as she ran a hand over his head.

"It's a Mohawk, Nana."

"Oh, so you think you Mr. T now, huh?" she joked, causing them both to laugh.

"I'm so glad you came by, De'," Ms. Gloria said as she pulled him in for another hug. "You know how much I worry about you."

The hardened killer looked down in shame. No matter how ruthless he may have appeared to the streets, Gloria Wubbins would always be the warm part of his heart. Her condition just pained him to the point where it was easier to stay away.

"I'm sorry, Nana. It's just—"

"I know, darling. You hate seeing me like this. But it's life, De'. Sometimes things happen and you can either give up or continue fighting. And my faith in the good Lord allows me to continue."

Her last statement made him look away in bitterness. While he would never admit it to her, he blamed God for her affliction.

With a strung out mother and a father he wouldn't recognize if they were in the same room, Ms. Gloria had been D-Wub's legal guardian before he took his first steps. So, he was devastated when the decision was made to place her in a nursing home.

Taken in by an inattentive aunt who was in good health despite her ungodly ways, he would often ask God why his grandmother, who regularly attended church and paid monthly tithes, was forced to undergo such a helpless situation. It was shortly after when his hurt converted to anger and his heart began to freeze over.

In the midst of their reminiscing on better days, D-Wub suddenly announced that he had a surprise for her and left the room. He returned minutes later with Sade, the Golden Retriever he had used in connection with the robbery.

After introducing the two women, who immediately took to each other, he explained how Sade was a well-trained guide dog. "Now you can go for walks whenever you feel like it, Nana."

He sat and talked with her until she began to fall asleep. "I'll come back later, Nana," he said as he gently helped her to bed.

"I'm sorry, De'. I don't know what's wrong with me. I'm just so tired."

"Don't worry 'bout it, Nana. Just get some sleep."

"Okay, darling. But don't take so long to come back and see me, you hear?"

"Yes ma'am," he replied, then leaned down to kiss her cheek as he pulled the covers over her.

Pausing in the doorway, D-Wub turned back to look at the woman who loved him unconditionally and thought, *why her*? It was a question he had been asking himself for years.

Turning off his emotions as he climbed back inside his scarlet colored Hellcat, he hit Suge up while speeding away from the nursing home. "Meet me out east, gotti," he directed.

It was time to feed the wolves.

***

"Twenty when I go!" Young-Loc yelled as he slammed his last domino to the table.

"This nigga lucky as *fuck*!" Tooly complained

as he and J-Bo flipped over their remaining bones. "What the babies gon' do, Cuzz?" Young-Loc shot back. "Now quit cryin' an' count my shit up."

After two days of vibing heavily with both men, J-Bo could see that beneath their rugged exteriors were genuine soldiers who suffered from a lack of guidance. The trenches being all they knew, they saw no error in their heartless and immoral ways.

Later that day as J-Bo was in the middle of teaching them how to play chess, a deputy entered the tank and told him to pack it up. "Franklin County sheriffs are down in booking."

As they were exchanging hugs and farewells, J-Bo gave Young-Loc and Tooly, both fighting bodies, the type of counsel that only a real one would give. "Under no circumstances will we *ever* compromise our morals an' principles. Snitchin' is the tendency of a bitch nigga, but we going to our grave as *men*."

His chin up and eyes blazing with intensity, Young-Loc replied, "Ain't no *mystery*, Cuzz!"

Chapter 8

Settled in a corner booth in the back of Applebee's, Ciara was sipping on a lemon iced-tea when Bhomas swaggered into the restaurant smelling like straight gas. His attire predominantly red as usual, he wore an Ohio State toboggan over his braided dreads.

"What's poppin?" he greeted in a dry tone as he sat across from her and laid a strap beside him. After the body bag incident, it was S.O.S. on any Crip from Geer.

In response, Ciara wordlessly slid under the table and unfastened his pants. Then, placing an ice cube in her warm mouth, she started knocking him down on the slow side.

Falling victim to his lower desires, Bhomas ran a hand over his tattooed face before laying his head back against the seat.

Her neck game on point, Ciara had a mouthful of protein within minutes. Using a napkin to spit into, she came from under the table and licked her lips. "Mmm, you taste good."

The spell now broken, Bhomas waved her off. "Bitch, you pro'ly told that nigga Jinx the same thang."

This nigga a lame for real, Ciara smirked to herself. But regardless of his flawed character, she had to remain in chess player mode, which meant outthinking her opponent.

"Bhomas, I didn't call you here to discuss no other nigga *or* what happened the other night. I just wanted to apologize an' say that I'm sorry for bein' inconsiderate of your feelings. But like I told you, I got bills to pay. So, until I'm in a committed relationship with a stable man, then I gotta do what I gotta do.'' Playing further on his emotions, she reached out and grasped his hands affectionately. "An' I was hopin' that with you being a real one, you could understand where I'm comin' from."

"But I'm sayin' though, Blood. If you needed somethin' that bad, you coulda just told me. Not go fuck wit' a nigga from the other side."

"You right, baby. Now tell me what I gotta do to fix it."

His answer was exactly what she predicted it would be. "That nigga Jinx gotta go."

Before Ciara could respond, Bhomas got a call from Ghost. With his eyebrows drawn together as he listened intently, he was reaching for his strap before the call ended. "A'ight, Blood. I'm on my way."

"Aye, I gotta roll," he told Ciara as he shoved the gun back down in his pants. "But don't forget what I said."

"What's goin' on, Bhomas?'' she asked as if genuinely concerned.

"Call of duty."

As she watched him leave the restaurant and hop inside a gold Seville, she picked up her phone and dialed a familiar number.

When Neicy picked up several rings later, Ciara began, "I need you to promise me somethin'."

***

In a minivan with stolen tags and sliding doors on both sides, Bhomas, Moo-Moo, and Ghost were lurking in the parking lot of Franklin Park mall.

A bust down from the north named Quita had been on her lunch break when she spotted Eli and another active Crip named Homicide leaving Foot Locker. Wanting to impress Ghost, while also harboring hatred toward Eli for once rejecting her, she had notified him immediately.

While waiting for the next text, Ghost kept glancing up front at Moo-Moo who was behind the wheel. He could tell there something on his man's mind, but now was not the time. "Aye, Moo-Moo?"

"What's poppin'?" he answered without turning around. Light-skinned with long dreads and a wiry frame, he resembled a younger version of Bob Marley.

"I'm sayin', Blood. Whatever it is, push that shit to the side for right now. We finna get it in, homie."

Quita's text came minutes later. *They were leaving out through J.C. Penny.*

Loaded down with shopping bags, Eli and Homicide were discussing the upcoming weekend as they left the mall. Having already reserved a suite for two days, they and their girls were taking a trip up to Cedar Point, an amusement park in Sandusky, Ohio. Unaware of the venomous eyes watching them from across the lot, they jumped in Homicide's 2012 Mustang and skirted out.

Moo-Moo was trailing them from several cars back when Ghost suddenly spoke up. "Get in front of these niggas, Blood. They dead at the next light." Broad day or not, he refused to let them get away on some fluke shit.

Eli was playing DJ inside the Mustang as Homicide left-handedly steered them down Monroe. The lead car in the right lane, he was turning at the next light and jumping on the E-way. The supercharged Shelby would have them back in the hood within minutes.

"Stupid bitch!" Homicide exploded as a minivan suddenly cut in front of him at the last minute and slammed on its brakes. When the driver hit his right turn signal, Homicide lowered his window in anticipation. He couldn't wait to curse out whoever it was inside.

Eli's eyes swelled in fear when he saw a ski-masked gunman pop out of the van's passenger side. "Oh *shit!*" he uttered right before he pushed his door open and got loose.

Fop! Fop! Fop! Fop! Fop! Fop! Fop!

Bhomas fired multiple rounds at Eli as he ran in between cars and dashed across the busy intersection. He fell once when he reached the other side, then quickly sprung back up and hobbled into a jewelry store.

Homicide's situation, however, played out entirely different. Rather than run, he boldly reached toward his center console, where he kept a loaded Taurus. He was coming out with the semi' when Ghost stuck the barrel of his .44 Revolver inside the window and stated, "This Y.G. Ghost from Crenshaw Mafia, Blood," Then fired several head shots.

Boom! Boom! Boom!

As Ghost and Bhomas jumped back inside the

van, Moo-Moo was bending the corner before they could fully close their doors.

Super geeked by the fact that he had just R.I.P.'d a high-ranking opp', Ghost tilted his head back and howled in a perfectly-pitched tone, "Soo Wooooo!"

**

St. Vincent's Hospital

There were dozens of tear-stained faces at the hospital as Homicide's family members mourned his death. The brazen killing naturally gained the attention of the news media, his grieving mother explaining to a cameraman how much of a good boy he was and how she couldn't understand why anyone would want to hurt her baby.

"Darren would give you the shirt off his back. So for someone to kill him in cold blood like this just doesn't make any sense."

Aware of Homicide's gang affiliation, a few members of the family had to look down as his mother made him appear angelic. They were certain he'd placed quite a few other mothers in the same position as his own.

Meanwhile, in a hospital room on the third floor, Eli and his girl Keedra were talking when a doctor entered the room with a blank expression. "I have good news and news you may find unpleasing. The good news is that you suffered only a minor graze and will soon be released. The other news is that there are two detectives in the hallway who are quite anxious to speak with you."

"Damn, doc. Tell 'em I'm gone off the Percs right now an' can't talk."

"Mr. Turnbow, short of death, I don't believe there is anything that will prevent these men from seeing you."

With hardened expressions that came from combative years in the field, Detectives Miller and Cavanaugh entered the room in hooded sweatshirts and black fatigues. Both men of average height and muscular builds, but it was Cavanaugh who took the lead.

"I'm Detective Cavanaugh with the Gang Task Force and I'd like to ask you a few questions."

"Gang Task Force?" Eli repeated with a confused expression. "I don't know shit 'bout no gangs. Never banged in my life."

Miller cut in with a smirk. "So I guess your childhood friend isn't Kamauri Hunter AKA Shooter? Active member of the Geer Gang Crips."

Eli blinked before looking away. "I don't know 'im."

Cavanaugh turned to Keedra. "Ma'am, could we please have a minute alone with Mr. Turnbow?"

Keedra shook her head and replied, "I don't think that's a good idea, officer." Then, with a look of distrust, she added, "You know... for the safety of my man."

Top heavy with a handful in the back, Keedra was light brown with freckles and shoulder length hair. A firecracker who was also a native of Geer hood, it was a mystery to no one as to who controlled the wheel of her and Eli's relationship.

Cavanaugh shrugged at her wanting to stay in the room, then moved in closer to Eli's bed. "Here's what I think. The Bloods initiated this gang war through the shooting out at the Hawthorne hotel. The Crips retaliated with the body bag killings, then today the Bloods got some revenge."

Unshaken by the detective's intense stare, Eli responded, "Here's what I think. I don't know *shit* about *shit*. So either cuff me up or get the fuck out my room!"

Kweli

Chapter 9

Hiding out in a hut out east, Ghost, Moo-Moo, and Bhomas were settled in front of a 60-inch as channel eleven news covered the story of Homicide's execution. Unremorseful of his death, their only concern was whether or not officials had any leads.

After glancing at his phone for the hundredth time, Moo-Moo stubbed out his square and stood up. "Aye, I gotta slide to the crib real quick," he announced, while tucking a SIG on his waist. "I'ma get up wit' you niggas tomorrow." He shook up with both men and left out through the back.

Ghost looked at Bhomas, who shrugged in response.

Climbing inside his '09 Beamer, Moo-Moo put his strap under the seat, then fired up another 'Port and laid his skully against the headrest. At only eighteen, he could feel the weight of the world on his shoulders.

As he was reaching for the gearshift, the passenger door suddenly opened and Ghost slipped into the car. Moo-Moo's perceptive eyes instantly noticed the concealment of his right hand. He thought about the SIG, but knew reaching for it would be pointless. And besides, if Ghost wanted him dead, he'd already be dead.

"You makin' me nervous, homie," Ghost said as Moo-Moo settled back in his seat. "Got me thinkin' shit I'on even like thinkin'."

Placing himself in Ghost's shoes, Moo-Moo knew if roles were reversed, he too would be having the same speculations. But like any real one would do, he defended his integrity. "I ain't got no breakin' point, gotti, an' you *know* that." He was referring to a situation when he had been picked up for questioning in regards to a murder he and Ghost actually committed. Interrogated and threatened for six hours straight, he had literally spoken only four words, "Where my lawyer at?"

As the two young savages held each other's stare, Moo-Moo could sense this was an instance when honesty would outweigh all else. So, not wanting to force Ghost's hand, he broke the stare and began to reveal the cause of his distress.

"I got to the crib last night an' found my lil' brother hidin' under his bed. When I got 'im to come out, I see he got bruises all over back an' shit. An' when I asked him who did it," Moo-Moo paused to hit the squally, "My lil' nigga *peed* on his self."

He turned to face Ghost and admitted, "Shit fucked me up, gotti. That he could be that scared, you feel me? An' that's why I kept checkin' the time on my phone like that. I ain't had a chance to bump into my dope fiend-ass momma, so I'm just tryna get to crib an' see what fuck goin' on." The caretaker of his eight-year-old brother, Moo-Moo had been forced to step up at an early age.

A moment of silence lingered inside the car before Ghost offered his chilling perspective. "You been givin' yo' moms too many passes, homie. You need to apply some pressure. Otherwise, shit gon' get *much* worse fa lil' bra."

"But this my momma we talkin' 'bout," Moo-Moo said in her defense.

"Nah, homie," Ghost disagreed with a headshake. "You seein' it wrong. The word momma ain't shit but a title. That's it. Just 'cause she yo' momma don't mean she gon' give a fuck about you. You gotta start seein' Charlene for who the fuck Charlene is. Fa real, Blood. Ain't no room for emotions in a world like this."

Before exiting the car, Ghost removed his right hand from his coat pocket and shook up with Moo-Moo. "My apologies, homie."

During his drive to the North, Moo-Moo was in deep thought as "Dream Chaser's 2" played inside the car.

"Stunting every chance I get because I had it poor. But every time I go to sleep I see the devil at my door…. Mommies turn to zombies from that raw, because its crack galore. You wonder why them babbies runnin' crazy steady clappin off…"

Meek Mill's hit single "The Ride" mirrored Moo-Moo's thoughts.

***

With a rubber string still tied around her arm and a syringe lying on the couch, Charlene and her current man, Eddie, were in a deep nod when Moo-Moo stepped inside the house. This being a typical scene, he was unaffected by her condition.

Deciding he would cut into her later, Moo-Moo went upstairs to his brother's room. His eyes instantly went from the empty bed to a dresser that was pushed up against the closet door. Moving it aside, he opened the door to find his little brother asleep on the floor.

"Boogie!"

His eyes shot open in fear.

"Charlene did this?"

When he didn't answer, Moo-Moo snatched him up and repeated, "Did Charlene do this?"

A tear fell from his eye as he slowly nodded.

Enraged, Moo-Moo flew back downstairs and smacked fire out of her and Eddie. "Get the fuck up!"

"Boy, what the fuck is yo' problem?" Charlene demanded, her eyes blinking rapidly as she rubbed her stinging cheek.

Recovering from the initial shock of being slapped awake, Eddie rose up from the couch in a threatening manner. "I know you ain't just put yo' muthafuckin' dick-beaters on me."

Moo-Moo pulled out the SIG and held it down at his side. "That ain't all I'ma do if you don't sit yo' bitch-ass back down."

Eddie sneered, "That gun make you a big man, huh?"

Moo-Moo thumbed the hammer back in response.

A menacing glare in his eyes, Eddie slowly nodded as he reluctantly took a seat.

"Why Boogie got bruises all over his back?" Moo-Moo heatedly questioned his mother. "An' what the fuck he doin' locked in a closet?"

Charlene shook a G.P.C. out of a nearly empty pack and fired it up. "I don't gotta explain *shit* to you when it comes to disciplinin' my own child. An' if you don't like it, then you can get yo' shit and get the fuck out my house."

"Why won't you just sign the papers, then you ain't even gotta worry 'bout Boogie no more? You know you don't give a fuck about 'im." Since turning eighteen, Moo-Moo had been trying to convince her to sign over her parental rights.

"Tell you what," Charlene said after her and Eddie exchanged a knowing look. "Since you wont him so damn bad, then why don't you pay for the bastard."

"How much?'' Moo-Moo replied without hesitation.

"Twenty thousand an' you can have 'im."

"Twenty thousand?"

"Nigga, I know you out there slangin' that shit. So don't tryda stand here an' act like you can't get it. Matter fact, you gotta month to come up wit' it or I'm evictin' yo' punk-ass. An' if you tryda pull some slick shit, I'll call the police on you an' yo' lil' gangbangin'ass friends."

Protecting Boogie being the only reason he continued to live under her roof, Moo-Moo had no choice but to nod in agreement. "A'ight, but I'm tellin' you now. If I see anymore bruises on Blood, I'ma treat you like a stranger."

As he turned to go back upstairs, Charlene called out, "I think you should give me few hunid right now. You know, as a down payment."

Kweli

Chapter 10

Montego Bay, Jamaica

Exchanging light conversation under a starlit sky, Fat-Cat and Kiona held hands as they leisurely strolled down the beach at 3 a.m. Her hair twisted into Caribbean-styled braids, she flaunted her flawless figure in a Mara Hoffman two-piece, while Fat-Cat wore a plain Patek and Polo shorts.

Since their arrival at the Sandals Resort, they had went dancing to Caribbean music in overcrowded clubs, sailed into the turquoise-colored ocean aboard a glass bottom boat, and feasted on various seafood at a lobster buffet. And because money was not an issue, there was a lot more to experience over the following three days.

They claimed a section on the nearly vacant beach and laid a small blanket over the white sands. Then, removing a bottle of Dom Perignon and two wine glasses from a picnic basket, they toasted to a bright and successful future.

With one of her fantasies being to have sex among such a beautiful scenery, Kiona set it off with a slow and sensual kiss. Then, pushing him back, she drizzled champagne over his stomach and slurped it up.

Unconcerned with prying eyes, she pulled his boy out and slowly licked it from bottom to top before sliding down on him with a pleasurable sigh. Leaning over so he could nurse one her sensitive nipples, she noisily grinded herself into a seizure-like orgasm.

Kiona's legs on wobble, Fat-Cat carried her back to their room, where he gently ate the pussy until she passed out.

Later that afternoon as they rode in a cab on their way to Kingston, Kiona continued to express her concerns. "Baby, I'm tellin' you, I don't think this a good idea. You know they say niggas in Kingston be tryna rob American tourists."

"That's why I told you to stay in the room."

Kiona looked at him sideways. "So what, I'm just supposed to let you go by yo'self?"

Raised in a two-parent household out in the 'burbs, Kiona had grown up enjoying the benefits of a privileged life while also being exposed to the game. Her father, Freddie Coleman, had touched more bricks than a construction company. And wanting to have a daughter who could avoid the common pitfalls of so many young women, he held no punches when it came to educating her on life.

"Don't ever have dealings with a broke nigga," he'd schooled her shortly after she reached puberty. "It means he has no ambition. An' a nigga with no ambition is worthless. An' when the day comes that you do meet a thorough ass nigga, one that treats you as you've witnessed me treat yo' mother, then you make sho' you have his back at all costs."

Kiona and Fat-Cat were both amazed by the dramatic change of scenery as they entered the rural parts of Kingston. Now being driven down a narrow dirt road, they took in the rundown shacks that were considered houses and the pigs that carelessly roamed the area.

Minutes later, the cab driver pulled into a

neighborhood resembling something out of a third world country. Parking in front of a yellow shack, he told Fat-Cat and Kiona to stay put when a group of men standing outside the house began to approach. The cab driver quickly hopped out and raced around the car to cut them off. And even when he explained what he wanted, the men were still looking over his shoulders to see who was inside the car.

After a deal was struck, he motioned for Fat-Cat to lower his window. "Di money, mon."

He peeled off a fifty and passed it through the narrow opening.

The Jamaicans instantly began to feud over who would make the sale. Fifty American dollars went a long way.

As the cab driver hurried back around the car with a zip of kush, Fat-Cat locked eyes with one of the dreadheads. When he did, he was able to see beyond the heartless expression and into a painful struggle he could never imagine.

"Hol' up," he told the cab driver before he could pull off.

His head jerked around. "We must go, mon. Dem dangerous."

Her look a mixture of fear and confusion, Kiona asked, "What are you doin', Chris?"

"What real niggas do," he answered right before he surprised them both and stepped out of the car.

"My name Fat-Cat," he stated with clarity as he slid his gaze over each man. "I come from the struggle myself, but not one nearly as severe as yours."

Without a trace of fear in his heart, he reached in his pocket and pulled out a bankroll. Their wolfish eyes were magnetically drawn to his hand. "I ain't no better than you," Fat-Cat continued. "I was just fortunate enough to grow up in America." Having already identified the alpha of the group, he turned to him and held out the money. "Not out of sympathy but out of respect."

Real recognizing real, the Jamaican whose name was Graveyard, accepted the donation and gave Fat-Cat a firm handshake. "Respec', rude boi."

Sliding back down into the car, Fat-Cat saluted Graveyard and his men as the cab driver pulled away from the curb. "Now let's smoke," he said before leaning over to kiss Kiona on the cheek.

Chapter 11

A 30-round semi lying within arms reach, Suge was in Neicy's kitchen turning two of the seven bricks he'd received from D-Wub into four. After one of his J's had instantly OD'd off of a tester, he knew the heroin could take a "one" and still be fire enough for others to have wiggle room. He would ensure the Wolf Pack was known for distributing quality work.

Wearing a gas mask and rubber gloves, he moved with an efficiency that came from experience. Suge was inwardly geeked by the idea of seeing a mill' ticket. It made him think of his mans, Boob-Mac, whose ambition had been similar to his own. But unfortunately, he had allowed greed to be his downfall.

Brown skin with a wavy taper and six slugs on the bottom, Suge had a hustle-hand that some would consider a gift from above. It was for that reason, along with his unquestionable loyalty, that D-Wub had appointed him lieutenant. "I trust you, gotti," he'd told him after handing over the seven bricks. "So while I take this trip o.t., I need you to feed the team an' act as overseer." Asking no questions in regards to where the heroin came from, Suge assured D-Wub that failure was not an option.

After a thorough cleansing of the makeshift lab, Suge was stacking compressed nine packs into a duffel bag when Neicy entered the kitchen in terry cloth boy shorts and a beater with no bra. Ass dumb-fat and D-cups sitting up invitingly.

"Good morning, bae," she greeted as she draped

her arms around his neck. Her smooth skin the color of cinnamon, Neicy was a dime in any man's opinion.

"What's good, ma?" he inattentively replied, while continuing to load the bag.

"Why you ain't come wake me up? You know this my off day."

"I ain't got time."

Stung by his answer, Neicy shot back with sass, "But you got time to come over here an' do this shit in my kitchen though, huh?"

Now playing in a different league, Suge refused to get sidetracked by anything. Pussy included. He pulled out a bankroll and counted off two bands. "Here. Go buy yo'self somethin' for the weekend an' we gon' go out."

She shook her head in refusal and replied, "You think givin' me money an' buyin' me shit is enough, but it ain't, Suge."

After faithfully playing the sideline for nearly a year, Neicy had done everything possible to prove that she was worthy of a relationship. But lately, she was beginning to wonder if giving him the keys to her house and her heart had been a mistake.

Suge laid the money on the countertop and picked up the bag. "I can't do this wit' you right now, Neicy." At twenty-three and a promising future now looming ahead, chasing a ticket was the only commitment he was interested in.

As Neicy watched him leave from her bedroom window, she sadly thought to herself, *Please don't make me change the locks, Suge.*

***

Not knowing how long he'd be out of town, D-Wub went back to Safe Haven to spend the day with his grandmother. After going out to eat and for a walk through Pearson Park, they went back to her room where he patiently sat with her until she dozed off.

He purposely bumped into Ms. Phyllis on his way out and pulled her aside. "I appreciate you being close friends with my granny," he said as he removed what she considered a fortune and slid it to her with discretion.

She gratefully tucked the roll inside her bra with a promise that she would always make sure Ms. Gloria was comfortable. This was a ritual they'd been following for several years now.

Before leaving town, D-Wub had to stop by his crib to pick up Bella. As he was turning into the parking garage of his studio apartment, six black-on-black Escalades suddenly came out of nowhere and boxed him in. Wearing tailored suits and fierce expressions, eleven Asians hopped out with submachine guns.

Appearing to be in his late forties, a twelfth man who was unarmed, stepped between two of the assassins and signaled for D-Wub to get out.

His palms sweating as he clutched a 30-round Ruger, he courageously complied. "What's poppin', Blood?"

"De'Angelo Wubbins," the Asian spoke in perfect English. "Your grandmother is Gloria Wubbins who currently resides at Safe Haven

Nursing Home in room 116. Has a golden retriever you recently bought her named Sade. Primary caretaker, Phyllis Cunningham."

Despite D-Wub showing no physical reaction, the man's intimate revelation gave him chills. He thought shit like this only happened in movies.

"I will only ask you once," the Asian continued. "Where the *fuck* is Darius Miller, or as you may know him, Kool-Aid?"

D-Wub smirked before answering, "In a cemetery."

This being information he already knew, his next question was one he didn't have an answer to, "By whom?"

"*Me*," D-Wub confessed with emphasis. "Bitch ass nigga was a rat."

"That *rat* owed me a quarter-mill'." The Asian being a high-ranking member of the Triads, it was his son who had been Kool-Aid's plug. They had crossed paths at a Lakers game out in L.A.

The assassins' grips tightened on the Uzis as D-Wub stepped closer to their leader. "I fear nothin' in this world," he coldly stated as they stood only inches apart. "Not even the death of my granny. But on the strength of my respect for good business, I'll see to it that you're fully compensated."

"And exactly how long will this take?"

He was genuinely surprised when D-Wub answered, "Tomorrow."

After agreeing to meet at an Asian restaurant called Panda's, the Triad leader and his soldiers climbed back inside the ESVs and left just as quickly as they'd came.

***

"Dadyyyyy!" Ciara screamed out as Big-Mike manhandled her from the back. Looking over her shoulder as she met him thrust for thrust, she told him, "Punish this pussy!"

As he avoided focusing on her jiggily cheeks, Big-Mike latched on to her expensive sew-in and did as requested.

Taking it like a champ, Ciara tightened her vaginal muscles, then eyed him through the mirror in front of the bed and yelled, "Open yo' eyes while you fuckin' the shit outta me!" When they blinked open, she replied, "Look how you got this fat ass clappin' all over that dick."

Her words along with the heated moisture of her snot box being too much for him to bear, Big-Mike tried to force all 265 pounds of himself into Ciara as he came with an high-pitched wail.

Breathlessly lying side-by-side on the bed, Ciara took a moment to stroke his ego before she grabbed her clothes and stumbled to the bathroom.

Still naked, Big-Mike was propped up on his elbows cheesing when Ciara came out fully dressed with her iPhone in hand. "Girl, we gotta do this more often. You already know a band ain't *shit* to a nigga like me." A brick-boy from the Weiler Home projects out east, Big-Mike was an older cat who had been getting money for years.

Ciara stepped closer to the bed and held the phone up so he could see the screen.

Leaning forward, his eyebrows bunched into a

confused frown when he saw the numbers 911.

"If I touch this screen," Ciara said as her thumb hovered over the green display, "Then you already know what's next. Whether I hang up or not, them boys on the way."

"Fuck is you gettin' at?" Big-Mike growled.

"I'm givin' you two hours from the moment you leave this room to get me twenty-five thousand or I'ma call the police and tell 'em you raped me."

He furiously flew up off the bed. "Bitch—"

Ciara stepped back and pulled out a potent can of pepper spray. "This hotel got cameras everywhere. There's even one right outside in the hallway. So you may wanna think twice before you do somethin' you'll end up regrettin'."

"You triflin'ass hoe."

Ciara sneered, "You beat the pussy up good, too, Big-Mike. So, you can only imagine what the results of a rape kit would be. Your choice, twenty-five racks, or a twenty-five year sentence."

Not only was Big-Mike hood rich, but Ciara also knew the fat nigga was soft as cotton. He would most likely keep this incident to himself out of embarrassment. But in the event that he did decide to put a comma on her head, with her and Neicy leaving in two weeks, she'd be safely tucked away in Atlanta by then.

Eyeing her with a venomous stare as he got dressed, Big-Mike assured her he would return to the hotel with the money. "But karma gon' get you," he condemned her on his way out.

Ciara closed the door behind him thinking to herself, *It already did.*

***

His phone rolling already, Suge was lining up multiple plays as he punched the SRT8 out to Holland Sylvania. He'd already blessed Ghost, Bhomas, and Moo-Moo with half bricks apiece, along with specific instructions. "We already known for drillin' shit, gotti. Now let's be known for gettin' money."

With five whole ones on tuck and D-Wub assuring them there would be more on the way, Suge was anxious to handout his first "M".

On his way to drop off a nine-pack to his young hooli' Turk, who was eager to become a member of the Wolf-Pack, Suge realized he hadn't ate all day and stopped at a Wendy's. The drive-thru line super long, he double parked the Challenger and ran inside.

Wolfing down a double stack as he came back out, Suge felt a presence to his left and turned.

"Gimme the keys!" a hooded man in dark shades and a blue bandanna barked as he shakily held a chrome .357.

This scary ass 'bout to shoot me, Suge nervously thought to himself as he stood frozen.

The gunman poked the barrel into his temple, "Hurry up, bitch ass nigga!"

When he tossed the car keys on the ground, another man picked them up before running his pockets and taking a Cuban Link from around his neck. Then he swung a vicious hook that put Suge on his ass.

"You shoulda let me drill that nigga, Cuzz," Suge heard the gunman say to his accomplice as they fled.

Staggering back to his feet, Suge helplessly watched as they scratched off in the Challenger with two and a half bricks in the backseat.

Chapter 12

Franklin County Jail

"Here's a copy of your Motion to Discover," J-Bo's lawyer, Mr. Letner, said as he removed a small stack of papers from his bag. An older white man with a vicious hump and nicotine-scented clothes, he was one of the two lawyers assigned to his capital case.

After standing before a judge and pleading not guilty to all forty-seven counts of his indictment, J-Bo was again denied bond, then calmly listened as the prosecutor informed the court that they were seeking the death penalty. While he was suspected of being responsible for the bombing of the police station, there had been nothing concrete enough for a grand jury to indict him on.

With no choice but to provide the indigent defendant with legal assistance, the judge had appointed two washed-up lawyers from the public defender's office; a game J-Bo clearly understood. Their allegiance would belong to those responsible for signing their paychecks.

The handcuffs making it difficult to flip through his discovery, J-Bo asked Mr. Letner if he'd already read over it.

"I did actually. Just before coming over."

His next question was one he'd been unable to answer since the night of his arrest. "How did I become a suspect?"

Mr. Letner looked down at the discovery and shook his head. "There's nothing in here that mentions anything about that. But it does state that when you stopped at the gas station, you were spotted by someone who apparently decided to collect the ten thousand reward for your arrest. So, they contacted the police, then while staying on the line, simply followed you." He thumbed through the report until he found a certain page and turned it around.

When J-Bo looked down and saw the name, his eyebrows rose in genuine surprise. The Judas was Ciara. The same Ciara who thought he had chalked her for her cut from the lick in Detroit. She had been the person inside the red CTS who followed him from the gas station that night.

After seeing his face broadcasted all over the news, along with the $10,000 reward for his arrest, Ciara couldn't believe her luck when J-Bo pulled up to the pump in front of her and hopped out.

Shoulda broke bread, nigga, she spitefully thought to herself while reaching for her phone.

J-Bo had never intended to chalk her, but with so much going on at the time, hitting her mitt had completely slipped his mind. Now it was possible his failure to tie up one loose end could unravel his entire life.

"Mr. Bowden, the decision is yours but in a case of this magnitude, I highly recommend that we pursue a good plea deal."

J-Bo smirked. "Nah, I'm straight."

"Well, it seems Olivia's father, Dr. Patterson, has a great deal of influence with some pretty influential people. The prosecutor recently brought it to my attention that if you're willing to tell them where her body is, they're willing to negotiate. It's something you may want to consider."

"Negotiate what, life without parole? You think I'ma willingly cop out to some shit like that?" He leaned forward, staring directly into the man's eyes. "Go back an' tell 'em I don't know *shit* 'bout nobody. So get that needle ready".

Mr. Letner threw his hands up in frustration. "Hey, it's your life. If you—"

Knock! Knock! Knock!

A deputy cracked the door open and stuck his head inside. "Bowden, just hang tight after this. There's someone else here to see you."

"Wait a second, dep," Mr. Letner quickly spoke up as he began gathering his things. "It's getting late and I still have another client to see." Without a glance in J-Bo's direction, he said he would see him soon and hurriedly fled the room.

While watching him leave, J-Bo couldn't help but entertain thoughts of defeat. *How the fuck I'm supposed to win wit' somebody like him?*

Minutes later, a well dressed older black man was escorted into the room. He extended his hand as the deputy was closing the door. "I'm Philip Wingate."

"No offense," J-Bo said as he made no effort to reach out. "But I don't shake hands wit' cops."

Wingate lightly chuckled as he drew his hand back and brushed imaginary lint from his Armani suit. "Young man, I'm *far* from a cop. In fact, I'm the police and prosecutor's worst enemy. In my thirty-year career as a defense attorney, I can count my losses on one hand. And I've defended some of the most *notorious*."

Although his spiel held a ring of truth to it, J-Bo maintained a poker face. "So why you here?"

"Terry Jones," he answered as he took a seat and crossed his legs in a naturally smooth manner. Ignoring J-Bo's shocked reaction, he continued.

"He called me a few days ago and explained how you needed the help that only someone like myself could provide. Him, being an old friend and all, I assured him I would do what it took to ensure that you came out on top. And *that's* why I'm here."

Phillip Wingate was indeed a legendary lawyer from Detroit that Terry Jones kept on retainer back in his heydays. Armed with a competitive spirit and the gift of charisma, he had established a solid rep' as a trial lawyer who enjoyed winning just as much as his clients.

Acting as if he was looking for something inside his coat pocket, Wingate intentionally avoided eye contact with J-Bo as he explained how Terry Jones could provide him with a solid alibi on the day of the bank robbery.

"But first I need you to think about if there's any way they'll be able to discredit the testimony of this witness. 'Cause once they're on that stand, there's no turning back."

An alibi? J-Bo was speechless for a second, but quickly recovered. "Nah, they good. 'Cause I ain't have shit to do wit' no robbery an' ain't no way they can prove I done *ever* been to this city."

Wingate uncrossed his legs and sat up. "Well, in that case, I'll stop by the public defender's office when I leave here and tell them to file a 'motion to withdraw' as your appointed counsel. The judge will schedule a pre-trial hearing in a few days, and I'll see you then."

His demeanor nonchalant, J-Bo nodded.

"So do you have any questions?" Wingate inquired as they rose from the table.

As bad as J-Bo wanted to see the glass as half full, he had to face reality. "You know they caught me wit' the money, right?"

"First, the bills weren't marked. And secondly, I've read over the entire case and there's nothing connecting you to the crime scene. So let's say you *are* guilty of picking up a car with a trunk full of already stolen money. With our witness providing you with a solid alibi during the time of the robbery, you're looking at a 'receiving stolen property' charge."

Wingate saw the look of uncertainty in his eyes and placed a hand on his shoulder encouragingly. "I know it may seem farfetched right now, but I wouldn't take this case if I didn't think I could win. And to me, winning is all that matters."

When he extended his hand for a second time, there was no hesitation on J-Bo's part. And unlike Mr. Letner, Wingate's handshake was firm, which in most cases said something about a man.

The feeling of hopelessness that J-Bo usually felt after a lawyer visit was absent as he and Wingate parted ways. Beneath his calm appearance, his insides were bubbling with excitement. Terry Jones had put him back in the game.

Not only had he copped a savvy spokesman, but had also found someone willing to commit perjury.

While J-Bo knew a friendship between them could never exist, there was no denying that the man's actions were deserving of a certain level of respect.

His future suddenly looking bright, J-Bo smiled to himself as he was led back to his kennel. *I might can wiggle now!*

Chapter 13

Pulling the Hellcat into the parking lot of Panda's, D-Wub grabbed a bookbag off the passenger seat and hopped out. A glock .40 with armor piercers on his waist, he soldiered into the small restaurant where an older Asian woman stood behind the counter.

"Have a seat," she said as she motioned with her hand. "Mr. Lee be with you in one moment."

He chose to sit where the entire restaurant was visible, then laid the bag beside him with his trigger hand lying on his lap.

At precisely 2 p.m., which was their designated meeting time, Mr. Lee and two of his assassins emerged from the back.

D-Wub stood up as they approached.

"I assume you're a man of your word," Mr. Lee said.

D-Wub dropped the bag on the floor and kicked it towards him. "I added fifty to make it a even three-hunid," he said, then turned to leave.

"Wait!"

Beaming on the inside, D-Wub maintained his composure as he turned back around.

The Asian gangster studied him with sadistic eyes before asking, "How much can you handle?"

***

Foster's Barber Shop

Huddled inside a backroom of the shop, a group of brick boys from all over the city were loudly engaged in an invite only crap game where you couldn't touch the dice unless you were shooting $500 or better. There was an *easy* 100 grand inside the room.

"Bet a thousand I six-eight or seven-eleven!" Jinx barked as he angrily slung ten blue faces to the floor. He was down $7,700.

"Bet!" a light-skinned nigga named Juice eagerly called, dropping a variety of bills on the floor.

As thousands inside bets were being wagered, Jinx got down on one knee and shook the dice inside his closed hand. "You niggas can't break Jinx!" he loudly boasted. "I'll have a armor truck pull up to this bitch!"

He released the dice with a loud snap of the fingers and yelled, "Big Cs!"

The room got super loud when he rolled a five.

Still down on one knee, Jinx threw another pile of money on the floor and looked up at Juice. "Bet twenty-three hunid I nine-five."

His hands full of money and pockets on chubb, Juice arrogantly threw his fade money on the floor. "Roll, sweet ass nigga."

Jinx dropped the dice and popped straight up. "Watch yo' mouth, Cuzz. Don't ever call me out my name."

"Come on, bra," Juice replied with a smile, "You ain't gotta get in yo' feelings over this lil' shit. If you need a loan, just let me know."

After several tense seconds, Jinx smirked, then got back down to roll and crapped out.

As people were quietly scooping up their money, Jinx eased the tension inside the room by joking as he said, "What you niggas so quiet fo'? Ima be back soon as I get my shit cut. You know my money long like train smoke!"

As usual, the shop was packed when Jinx walked up front. "Paid in Full" was playing on a big screen while Boosie Badazz rapped reality through a surround sound system. Acknowledged by nearly everyone as he hopped right into a chair, his barber Rock draped a cape over him and asked, "What you do to 'em back there?"

"They hit me for a soft ten," Jinx answered with a shrug.

Rock let out a low whistle. If he had $10,000 right now, he'd open up his own shop.

Like Rock, half the barbers at Fosters had perfected their craft while either doing federal or state bids. The owner's reason for doing so was to not only give them second chances, but more importantly, to employ those familiar with the illegal activities that went on at his shop from which he received a decent percentage

Jinx was halfway through his haircut when he felt his phone vibrating. Reaching under the cape to grab it, he frowned at the image on his screen. It was a picture of Suge, who was attempting to FaceTime him through his Facebook page. *Fuck this nigga want?*

"Aye, hold up real quick, Rock," he said as he removed the cape and stepped outside.

"What's craccin?" Jinx said as he connected the call, careful to position himself to where his location was unknown.

"Aye listen, gotti. I know we from different sides, but me an' you ain't never personally had a problem wit' each other."

Jinx shrugged impatiently. "A'ight, so what you sayin', Cuzz?"

"I'm sayin' that shit yo' men took gotta come back. That's a loss I can't accept."

"Fa one, I don't know what the fuck you talkin' 'bout. An' two, if I did know, you *still* wouldn't get that shit back."

"So that's how you gon' play it?"

"Nah, that's how ya mans an' nem played it when they started this shit over that hoe, Ciara. Learn to keep yo' dogs on a leash an' you won't have these problems, Cuzz."

"You know, as bosses, I thought we could—"

"Ce safe out here, Loc," Jinx said. Jinx disconnected the call and went back inside. It was too late for white flags and truces.

After Rock finished his razor-lined taper, Jinx called Shooter as he was walking back to the dice game.

Shooter answered on the second ring. "What's craccin, big homie?"

Jinx smiled at the readiness in his voice. "You know where I'm at, Cuzz. Bring me twenty-five racks up here real quick. I gotta get my shit back."

Chapter 14

Cincinnati, Ohio

In the parking lot of a bar on the west side called The Nugget, Joe-Joe sat inside a '77 Bonneville as he waited for the arrival of an old friend. Besides occasional phone calls, the two hadn't saw each other in several years.

Sipping on a bottled water, Joe-Joe cracked a slight grin when the driver of a burgundy Denali pulled in beside him and lowered his window.

"Young Joseph!" the driver greeted with a genuine smile.

"Muthafuckin' D-Wub!" Joe-Joe laughed as they hopped out and strongly embraced.

Both men active members of the Blood Gang, they had met in Cuyahoga Hills, a notorious juvenile joint in Cleveland, Ohio. Despite being from opposite ends of the state, Joe-Joe once saw D-Wub fearlessly confront a group of G.D.s and decided to intervene. He respected strength.

"I'm wit' *him*!" he'd growled with intensity as he walked up and nudged his head at a man he didn't even know. The two gladiators fought back-to-back that day, forging a bond that would carry over into the outside world.

With only a small crowd present in the afternoon hours, Joe-Joe invited D-Wub inside the bar for a drink. After an hour of throwing back shots of Patron while catching up, D-Wub decided it was time to get down to business.

"How you livin' out here, Blood?"

Knowing what he meant, Joe-Joe truthfully answered with a shrug, "I'm doin' a'ight. But shit could be better."

D-Wub eyed him for a minute, then said, "I gotta plug, Joe-Joe. No middle man. An' I'm sayin', there's room for you if wanna come aboard." With him now having an unlimited supply, a bigger city meant a bigger profit.

His eyes blinking rapidly as they often did while collecting his thoughts, Joe-Joe denied the invitation. "While I wholeheartedly appreciate the offer, 'Wub, I gotta team to consider. We struggle together an' we gon' bubble together."

D-Wub smiled at his loyalty. "I would never ask a general to leave his soldiers behind."

Caressing his unshaven beard, Joe-Joe inquired, "What type of numbers we speakin'?" Standing at 6'1" with a cocoa-colored complexion and 360s, he was direct by nature.

"I'ma give you whole ones fa seventy-five. An' I can front you as many as you can move."

Staring D-Wub directly in his eyes while also relying on his intuition, Joe-Joe began to slowly nod his head as he concluded this was indeed the same soldier he'd once stood alongside on the front line.

"I fucks wit' you that *one way*," Joe-Joe explained with a passionate aggression. "So, me myself *personally*, I'm all the way wit' it. But first, let me bark at my dawgs an' make sho they ready to eat outta bigger bowls, as well."

As they were walking back outside to their cars, Joe-Joe looked at D-Wub and asked, "Wassup wit' that nigga, Kool-Aid?" Through his extensive prison ties, he had been the one to inform D-Wub of Kool-Aid's weakness.

"What the homie Lil Wayne say," D-Wub answered with a smile. "All rats must die. Even Master Splinter."

"Type shit," Joe-Joe said, smirking with a nod of approval.

As he and D-Wub parted ways with plans to link up the next day, Joe-Joe summoned his team to one of their duck-offs over in Price Hill. Parking the Bonny in back of the house, he went inside and found his young hooli' Smoke slaying a bust down on the living room couch.

Barely slowing down, Smoke glanced over his shoulder and lifted his head in acknowledgement. "What's good, big bra?"

"*Business*," Joe-Joe curtly replied before he spun on his heels and left the room.

Smoke instantly pulled out and told the girl to get her shit on and bounce.

Dark skin with minimal facial hair, cornrows, and the eyes of a young savage, the nineteen-year-old stood at only 5'6". But the size of his heart compensated for his lack of height.

Boss and his cousin Pistol pulled up shortly after. Both men light skin with tall wiry frames, Pistol was the more vocal of the two, while Boss was the deadly one who despised attention.

Already speaking highly of D-Wub in the past, Joe-Joe bypassed the sides and got straight to the main. "My nigga D-Wub in the city an' Blood in a position to change our lives. He already got my signature. But before I sign y'all up, I need you to understand *exactly* what's involved."

Joe-Joe went on to explain how D-Wub's safety was his primary concern, discretion was mandatory, and greed would not be tolerated. "Trust me when I tell you it's enough for everybody to get they bellies full."

Reaching out to shake up with Joe-Joe, Smoke was first to accept the invitation along with its terms. "Sign me up, Blood."

Boss quietly followed suit.

Pistol slithered out of left field. "I'm sayin' doe, like if this nigga really munching all like that, then why we don't just *take* that shit!? Why get only a piece when we can get the whole thang, you feel me? Fa real, Blood, fuck this *up north* ass nigga!"

"So it's fuck me too, huh?" Joe-Joe growled with a vicious snarl.

"Nah, never that. I'm just—"

"It's gotta be fuck me if you sayin' fuck bra," Joe-Joe cut him off with flared nostrils. "I already told you this a man I got *hella* respect fo'. I was willin' back then an' I'm *still* willin' to stand front line wit' this nigga. I don't give a fuck about that geographical ass shit you spittin' out. 'Cause how many niggas in the city done offered to give yo' starvin' ass a *crumb*?"

When Pistol didn't reply, Joe-Joe continued. "This up north ass nigga, as you call 'im, is not only willin' to put food on *my* plate, but yours, as well. So wit' you labelin' yo'self a real nigga, then how can you *possibly* not respect that?"

Slowly nodding his head in understanding, Pistol looked at Joe-Joe and apologized. "Yeah, you right, Blood. That's my fault. I can't let my hunger override my morals." When he extended his hand as a sign of good faith, Joe-Joe grilled him for a minute, then reached out and the two fluidly shook up.

"Embrace bra for the real one he is," Joe-Joe said as he slid his gaze over each man, allowing it to linger on Pistol. "He a shrewd nigga fa real an' the shit he standin' on rock solid."

***

Boss, Pistol, and Smoke were standing outside cheefing on a stick of gas when Joe-Joe pulled up to the crib with D-Wub trailing in the Denali.

Rocking a red and black Jordan tracksuit over matching sixes, D-Wub went around to the passenger side of the SUV and opened the door. When the all-black and bowlegged Bella leaped out, the three men fearfully stepped back with Pistol reaching toward his waist.

D-Wub peeped his movement. "On Blood, she don't bite unless I tell her to."

As Joe-Joe was making introductions, D-Wub closely studied their eyes while shaking up with each man. And experience allowed him to immediately sense an underlying dislike from Pistol, whose handshake didn't match his smile. There would be no hesitation if Pistol ever showed a sign of aggression.

"That's a big mu'fucka!" Smoke said in awe of the 100 pound dog as they were going inside the house.

Pistol smirked. "That's one of them show dogs."

"Bring yo' life savings an' whatever dog you wont to," D-Wub instantly spoke up. "An' see if she a show dog."

Inside the house, D-Wub took the floor as Bella sat beside him with alert eyes. "To get yo' phones punchin' over night, I'ma give each of y'all an ounce of fire to pass out. Give a tenth to every J you know. Let 'em see we got the rawest shit in the city. An' if anybody feel like we stepping on toes, then I'm assumin' everybody in this room already got one under they belt. 'Cause not only is the dope un-limited, but so is the artillery."

As Boss took in D-Wub's spiel, he could tell from his eyes, mannerisms, and overall aura, that Joe-Joe was right. *Yeah*, he concluded to himself with a subtle nod. *Blood a thorough nigga. An' a true barbarian.*

After dishing out their packs, Pistol and Smoke were riding through the city later that day when Pistol suddenly lowered the music. "You know I fuck wit' you that *one* way, Blood." Friends since middle school, he and Smoke were two local rappers who swore that if they ever made it to the industry, they would never allow the success to sever their bond.

Smoke took two short tokes off the blunt and replied, "An' the feelin' mutual."

"I'm sayin' doe," Pistol continued. "Between me an' you, I ain't feelin' this nigga D-Wub. Joe-Joe *foolin'* by even bringing 'im to the table. 'Cause

I'm tellin' you, Blood, somethin' ain't right wit' buddy. Call it intuition. So I'm sayin', like I say we take 'im up top, then bury his bitch ass behind the Faye." An apartment complex out in Westwood, the Faye was surrounded by a heavily wooded area that no doubt already housed a cemetery-full of bodies.

The wheels in his mind turning, Smoke thoughtfully replied, "Let's just watch Blood for a minute an' see if he take off his mask. 'Cause if he sour like you think he is, then it's only a matter of time before he show us a sign." He then turned to look at Pistol with those savage eyes. "An' that's when we crush 'im."

Kweli

Chapter 15

Back in Toledo

Paired up in separate cars, Moo-Moo, Ghost, Bhomas, and Turk were on the verge of making CNN news. Fully charged off Bars and Beans, they were stationed down the street from C. Brown funeral home, where they watched Homicide's family and friends go inside to pay their respects.

After waiting until the funeral was well under way, the four savages talibanned-up and placed mirrored shades over their eyes before pulling the hotboxes into the parking lot.

Quickly hopping out, they grabbed 30-caliber machine guns off the backseat and mounted them onto the hoods. Then, with Turk recording the incident on Facebook Live, they slapped 200-round drums into the fully auto's, braced the stocks against their shoulders and opened fire.

Doom! Doom! Doom! Doom! Doom! Doom! Doom! Doom!

It was a catastrophic scene inside the funeral home as the mini missiles bullied their way through the bricks and into human flesh. Some even going through Homicide's coffin. Amidst the piercing screams and chaotic scattering, the death toll mounted quickly.

When several people tried to escape out the front door, Ghost swung his rifle in their direction and literally shredded them apart.

Doom! Doom! Doom! Doom! Doom!

"It's real out here, Blood!" Turk yelled over the heavy metal music. "We knocking off whole *families!*"

After spitting out over 300 rounds in less than a minute, they tossed the 30s on the ground and hopped back inside the cars, leaving skid marks on the pavement as they slid onto Nebraska and smashed out.

The publicized massacre would gain millions of views in under an hour.

***

Coming out of a bar on the north side at one in the morning, Bhomas and Turk were semi tipsy as they walked back to the car.

"Damn, Blood," Bhomas complained as threw the Seville in drive and sped off. "I swear I'on feel like drivin' yo' ass all the way out to the sticks." Not only was his alcohol level way over the legal limit, but he was riding strapped.

"I told you my girl gotta go to work an' need me to watch the baby," Turk reminded him.

His baby momma, Angie, had texted him earlier saying the babysitter was sick and she needed him home in time for her to go to work. Because she rarely sweated him about anything, Turk knew it was only fair that he come through for her whenever the need arose.

His trunk slapping as he punched the Seville down Dorr Street, Bhomas cursed in aggravation when his gas light popped on. The gauge on E, he had no choice but to pull up into a B.P. "It's some pressure in the console," he told Turk as he was getting out. "Roll one up while I pump this shit."

When Turk reached inside the console and grabbed the weed, there was something shiny coiled beneath it that caught his attention. Picking it up out of curiosity, he began to eye it, concentrating as he tried to recall where he'd seen it before.

Then it dawned on him. This was Suge's chain. The same one that was taken from around his neck when he got hit for the two and a half bricks. *This nigga robbed Suge*, Turk thought to himself in disbelief.

He looked up just in time to see Bhomas walking to the car and quickly dropped the chain and weed back inside the console. Instantly sober, his heart was racing a mile a minute.

"Fire that shit up," Bhomas said as he climbed back inside the car and pulled off.

"I'm cool, Blood. I ain't even twist nothin' up. I just wanna go to the crib an' lay it down."

Bhomas cut his eyes at him, but said nothing as he turned the music back up.

As they were crossing the intersection of Dorr and Reynolds, Bhomas glanced in his rearview, then quickly turned onto a side street. "Aye, don't look back, but po-po was just behind us."

Stricken with panic, Turk looked back anyway. "I'on see no—" His words got caught in his throat as he turned back around and found himself staring down the barrel of gun.

When leaving the gas station, Bhomas had immediately felt the change in Turk's energy, but couldn't pinpoint the reason for it until he remembered he'd left the chain inside the console. He was now grateful that Turk hadn't rolled up the weed, which would've rocked him to sleep.

"I swear to God I ain't gon' say shit!" Turk pleaded with genuine fear in his eyes.

"I know you ain't," Bhomas coldly replied right before he squeezed the trigger and ruined the passenger side of his car.

After using a towel from the trunk to wipe off the windows, Bhomas let the passenger seat all the way back, then cautiously drove to a commonly used burial ground, the Maumee River.

Ciara being his motivation, Bhomas was determined to get his weight up by any means. And to him, what easier way than to target those within his inner circle? On the day Suge had blessed him with the half brick, he spotted the duffel bag lying on the floor of the backseat and saw an opportunity he couldn't resist.

"You holla at Moo-Moo an' nem yet?" he had casually asked Suge, laying the bait. When Suge answered that he was headed their way next, Bhomas waited until he pulled off and immediately called Roni, a Crip from X-Blocc hood who he secretly committed capers with in the past. "Mask up, Blood, I'm on my way."

When Suge had rolled up to Moo-Moo's spot in the Challenger, Bhomas and Roni were already down the street sitting low in a Coupe, eyeing their prey like starving buzzards.

As Bhomas watched his Seville slowly sink down into the water, an image of Roni suddenly flashed through his mind. Because he, too, was taking a nap somewhere at the bottom of the Maumee River.

Kweli

Chapter 16

Atlanta International Airport

From their vacation in Jamaica, Fat-Cat and Kiona flew to Atlanta, where she was on the verge of blowing his mind with several surprises he would never expect.

Foreign cars common on the streets of Atlanta, Fat-Cat had arranged for a chauffeured Bentley Mulsanne to be at the airport when they landed. Beluga-black over linen leather interior, they were ushered into the Bentley's rear sanctuary by an older gentleman of Hawaiian descent. Kiona gave him the address to a location on the west side, then snuggled into her man as the quarter million dollar sedan slid down Peachtree.

Pulling into a plaza on Bankhead Boulevard a short while later, Kiona tied a Hermes scarf over Fat-Cat's eyes before they exited the car. "Don't be tryna peek," she said as she led him toward a mid-size shop and unlocked its front door. When they stepped inside, she flicked the lights on, then removed the scarf and yelled, "Surprise!"

Fat-Cat was speechless as he took in the expensively designed barber shop. Done in a powder blue and chrome scheme, there were six Theo barber chairs settled over a tiled floor, flat screens mounted in each corner, and several rows of padded chairs for the waiting customers. This was clearly the work of professionals.

Courtesy of Fat-Cat, Kiona was already the owner of a successfully ran beauty salon back in

Toledo. Wanting to express her gratitude, while also steering him toward the business world, she had used the profits from her salon to buy him the shop. A ride or die who was genuinely in love with her man, Kiona would do whatever it took to prevent him from becoming a statistic.

"Do you like it?" she asked as she eagerly grasped his hands. She knew this was something he always wanted, but never found the time to pursue.

Still in amazement, Fat-Cat looked at her and smiled, "Hell yeah, I like it!" His love and respect for her had just rose several levels.

"I didn't give it a name," Kiona continued. "I'll leave that up to you. I just wanted to express my love and loyalty through *actions*, rather than words. Happy anniversary, bae."

Against his will, Fat-Cat lightweight teared up. Having endured a traumatic childhood, Kiona's love and support introduced him to unfamiliar emotions that warmed his insides.

Cupping her face in his hands, Fat-Cat looked deeply into her eyes and came straight from his heart. "My word as a man, Kiona, I will never lie to you about anything. Even if it means the possibility of losin' you. You will always come first an' I will use discretion in my moments of weakness. All I ask in return is that honesty be just as important to you as the memory of your father is."

Kiona nodded without hesitation. "I can do that. And my word as a woman, death is the only way I will ever physically leave you. So whether you're a boss in the world or an inmate in prison, I will always be by your side, holdin' it down with no complaints."

Kiona then reached inside her Prada clutch and came out with a small velvet jewelry box. She went down on one knee, opened the box to reveal a three-stone gold band, then looked up at Fat-Cat. "I love you more than life, Christopher Scott. Will you marry me?"

Fat-Cat blinked and a tear rolled down his cheek. Kiona made it all worthwhile. His head nodding as he bent down, he answered "yes", then grabbed her hair and crushed his lips into hers.

As they were walking back to the car hand-in-hand, Fat-Cat asked her how was he supposed to run the barber shop all the way from Toledo.

"I thought you'd never ask," Kiona answered with a smile.

She had the driver take them out to Stone Mountain, where she'd already put down a security deposit on a three-bedroom townhouse with two-and a half baths and a saltwater pool.

"I see you been a busy woman," Fat-Cat commented as she gave him a tour of the house.

"I'm just doin' what I was taught by my father, which is to be a good woman to my man. Or should I now say, fiancé."

Fat-Cat smirked. He could only imagine Jinx's reaction when he told him he would soon be a married man.

"But seriously, Chris. I know Toledo is all you've ever known, but you have to admit that you've outgrown it. At your level, you're like a shark swimming inside a pond, bae. An' it's only a matter of time before the wrong people take notice."

While Fat-Cat didn't respond, he knew she was speaking in reference to the feds, who now had a division in the downtown area. With Toledo being so small, a person of his caliber could only rotate for so long before an investigation occurred.

"I can sell my salon and open up one down here," Kiona continued in persistence. "You got your own barber shop now an' we're standin' inside a home I can see us raisin' a family in."

Her proposition appealed to Fat-Cat, but he still had his troops to consider. And he credited a large part of his success in the game to him remaining loyal to those loyal to him.

"I feel everything you sayin', Kiona. But at the same time, I can't just up and leave my men out there like that. I at least need enough time to set it up to where they can continue without me." Believing that a general was only as strong as his army, Fat-Cat added, "'Cause where would I be without 'em?"

Kiona shook her head in disagreement and countered, "No, Chris. Where would they be without *you*?"

Chapter 17

"Tell me all this aint over no *hoe*, Bhomas!" Suge heatedly demanded as they faced each other in a living room. Standing off to the side, Ghost and Moo-Moo were also present.

Bhomas looked at Suge as if he was offended by the suggestion. "Hell naw, this aint over no hoe. Them bitch ass niggas kilt Fred, Blood. *Facts.*"

Known for his love and loyalty to the Blood Gang, Fred was a young hooli' from the north who many feared but everyone loved. His death had brought tears to some of the most ruthless.

"How you know they did it?" There were a lot of rumors and speculation, but not even D-Wub had stumbled across anything solid enough to act upon. And he had genuinely loved Fred.

"I got into it wit' the nigga Jinx at that Gotti concert. An' when him an' the nigga Shooter walked off, I heard 'im laugh an' say, 'Do that dead-rag like we did Fred'."

His expression went unnoticed, but Ghost instantly frowned at his account of what happened that night. Because he had been watching Bhomas from a distance and saw something totally different. *What this nigga lyin' fo?* Ghost thought to himself.

"So wassup, is you fuckin' this hoe, Ciara?" Suge further questioned. He had already spoken to Neicy about it and she confirmed that Bhomas was infatuated with her girl. So to lie would be signing his own death certificate.

"Yeah, I be fuckin' her," Bhomas answered with a shrug. "But that ain't got shit to do wit' this."

Suge took a deep breath and worriedly massaged the bridge of his nose. He had been so excited when D-Wub put him behind the wheel. But now it felt as if he was losing control and on the verge of crashing.

After the funeral home massacre, which left thirteen dead, four in critical, and twenty-three wounded, the city had been quiet as a church mouse for several days now. Under direct pressure from the governor to find the monsters responsible, T.P.D. were heavily patrolling the streets, arresting any and everyone.

Suge had personally felt the heat when he was pulled over right after serving one of his Js a gram. Luckily he hadn't been riding with anything more, and was only taken in for driving without license.

To calm his nerves, Suge twisted up a stick of pressure and deeply inhaled the potent bud. He passed it after several tokes and addressed the three men. "Clearly the city too hot right now to be in traffic trapping off the phones. But to have our hand presentable when 'Wub come back, I want y'all to bust them halfs I gave you down into spanks an' bang 'em for twenty-two-fifty apiece. An' I don't give a fuck who it is, ain't no deals."

As they were leaving the house, Suge held Ghost back and looked in his eyes. "Wassup, Blood? Is that nigga Bhomas lyin' to me?"

Ghost held his stare for a minute before answering, "Blood a good man. Why would he lie?" Unable to see the treachery inside Bhomas' heart, he based his answer off his loyalty to the Gang, rather than what was in plain sight. A decision he would soon regret.

***

"Never been a stranger to homicide, my city full of gangbangas and drive-bys. Why do we die at an early age? He was so young but still the victim of a twelve gauge."

Banging Tupac's song "Pain" inside a small apartment on the west side, Blueface and two other active Crips, Duke and Cam, were blowing a bag of White Widow while playing Call of Duty. They were just passing time until nightfall, when they would slide to the north and drop at least one body per man. And behind the funeral home shooting, no one was off limits.

"I'm tellin' you, Cuzz," Cam reasoned as they played the game, "This shit like real—"

Bang! Bang! Bang! Bang!

The sudden knock at the door sent the three men reaching straight for a hammer.

Bracing a 100-round Chopper against his shoulder, Blueface motioned for Duke to lower the music, then yelled, "Who is it?"

"Shooter!"

After checking the peephole, Blueface snatched the door open. "Fuck is you knockin' like that fo', Cuzz?"

Shooter blew off into the apartment. "You niggas woulda heard me the first time if y'all ain't have the music up so loud."

Eli walked in behind him. "What's craccin, Cuzz?" he greeted Blueface, who said nothing in reply as he eyed him with a cold expression.

"Why you bring this nigga over here, Shooter?" Blueface asked, his gaze locked on Eli.

"Cause he a homie, that's why."

"Nah," Blueface shook his head. "This nigga ain't no homie. He a muthafuckin' *coward*. He left a real homie to die alone."

"What was he supposed to do, Face?"

"What was he supposed to do?" Blueface repeated as he looked at Shooter like he had lost his mind. "The same thang you, me, or any other real one woulda did, fought back! This nigga ain't fire one shot. He *ran*, Cuzz. So I'd appreciate if you got this goofy up outta here."

"Come on, Cuzz," Eli finally spoke up. "I know Homicide was yo' mans an' all, but you ain't gon' keep disrespectin' me."

"Or *what*, bitch ass nigga?" Blueface challenged as he sat the gun down and got up in his grill.

Eli took flight, swinging a crispy two-punch combo, but there was no power behind it.

Blueface shook it off and melted him with a straight right down the pipe. He ran down on Eli as he fell back into a closet door and cocked back.

Before he could tuck him in, Shooter shoved him out the way. "Watch out, Cuzz. That shit over wit'."

"*Nigga!*" Blueface spazzed as he ran up on Shooter.

As the two young bulls stood horn to horn, Duke and Cam got up to intervene. "Y'all niggas is *foolin'* right now. These Blood niggas done shot up the homie's funeral an' put the shit online. Our war wit' them, not each other."

Neither man wanting to back down, it took for Eli to grab Shooter. "Come on, Cuzz. Let's roll. Like you said, the shit over wit'."

When they hopped inside a black-on-black G.T.O. and skirted out, Shooter looked at Eli as he gripped the wheel. "Wassup, Cuzz. What you tryna do?"

Knowing the extent of his question, Eli didn't immediately respond. If he said he wanted to body Blueface, then he'd be dead before the sun rose. This is what Eli loved most about Shooter. The fact that he always had his back and never sided against him for no one. And it had been this way since grade school.

"I'm cool, Cuzz," Eli decided. "I fought the nigga an' I can live wit' the outcome." While he doubted he and Blueface would ever be cool again, he didn't feel the altercation called for murder.

They were on their way to Shooter's crib when he got a collect call from the county. He pressed zero without hesitation. "What up?"

"What's craccin', Cuzz?" Young-Loc greeted in an energized tone. "I hear the city turnt up right now." This was his way of indirectly saying he had heard about the war.

"It'll blow over in a minute," Shooter assured him. "You know how the Blue team roll."

"*Wassup*, lil' ass nigga!?" Tooly playfully barked into the receiver as he took the phone from Young-Loc.

Shooter laughed and said, "I see yo' ugly ass got jokes."

"Nah, nigga. You the one wit' jokes. Commissary Monday an' you ain't dropped that bread off yet!"

"Damn, that's my fault, Cuzz. On Geer, I forgot. Matter fact—" he told Eli to shoot downtown to the county real quick. "Aye, I'm 'bout to have Eli bring me down there right now."

Young-Loc and Tooly, who had now been in the county for eight months, were well taken care of. Fat-Cat had paid over $60,000 in lawyer fees, Jinx dropped a bag off to their baby mommas on a monthly basis, and Shooter ensured that they went to commissary every week. Their solidity deserved nothing less.

After putting the max on both of their accounts, Shooter was leaving the county when he spotted a familiar face coming out of a bondsman office across the street.

Please don't let this nigga see me, he thought to himself as he quickly put his head down. He glanced up just as he was reaching for his door handle and knew he'd went unnoticed.

"Look at Cuzz walking to the white truck across the street," he told Eli in a hurried tone as he reached under his seat and came up clutching a FN with a 50-round drum.

In a red Maxes and a Bulls hoodie, it was Bhomas. When he walked around to the driver's side of the Avalanche, neither Eli or Shooter could believe their eyes. On the back of his hoodie was a picture of Shooter. And beneath it were the words,

"R.I.P. Shooter." Bhomas was celebrating a kill he hadn't even committed yet"

''Get behind this nigga," Shooter ordered as he anxiously click-clacked one in the head. "An' soon as we get from downtown, pull up next to 'im."

As they were coming up Adams, the Avalanche made a sudden right turn without using its blinker, then an arm extended out the back window and started firing directly at the G.T.O.

Fop! Fop! Fop! Fop! Fop! Fop! Fop!

Eli quickly swerved into the oncoming lane and sped around the car in front of him, barely avoidng a head on collision with a U-haul. The tires screaming as he slammed on the brakes and cut the wheel, he drifted the muscle car onto a side street and floored it. Banging another right two blocks down, they caught the Avalanche as it sped down Woodruff and pulled in behind it.

As the souped up G.T.O. quickly closed the gap, Shooter lowered his window, switched the FN to semi, then leaned out the car.

Boc! Boc! Boc! Boc! Boc! Boc! Boc! Boc!

Shattering the truck's back window, two of the hollows hit the opp' in the backseat, while one struck Bhomas in the shoulder, causing him to lose control of the wheel. When he tried to slam on the brakes, the truck fishtailed before loudly smacking a parked car.

Tying a T-shirt over his face as Eli skidded to a stop, Shooter immediately hopped out.

When the passenger pushed his door open and staggered out of the truck, Shooter stopped his heartbeat with three chestshots. As he got up closer on the truck, he saw a body lying on the backseat and the driver's door open. Instantly, he got low and crept around the back of the Avalanche. Peeking around it, he saw a blood trail on the ground and knew Bhomas had gotten away. But he was wounded.

I'm on yo' ass boy, Shooter smiled to himself.

He was turning to leave when he heard a moan of pain come from inside the truck. He opened the back door to find the opp, who had fired out the window lying facedown on the seat, literally crying tears. "I can't feel my body." The two hollow points had paralyzed him from the neck down.

"Don't worry, Cuzz. I ain't gon' kill you," Shooter joked with an amused grin. "Cause you ain't even a factor no mo'."

He pivoted toward the Pontiac, took several steps, then turned back around. "Nah, you might tell," Shooter told the opp before he put the gun to his head and turned his dome into a stadium.

Chapter 18

With her head on his chest, Suge and Neicy were lying in her California King watching a movie on NetFlix. While his eyes were on the screen, his thoughts were on the streets. With two more dead and Bhomas laid up with a severe shoulder injury, he had no choice but to inform D-Wub of his failure as a lieutenant. He still had the five bricks hidden in Neicy's basement, but it was pointless pulling them out with his men engaged in constant warfare.

As if the universe could sense his reluctance in calling D-Wub, his phone suddenly vibrated on the nightstand. He took a deep breath after peering at the screen, then slid from under Neicy and left the room.

"What up, gotti?" he greeted in a dry tone as he connected the call.

"What's poppin', Blood? You don't sound too happy to hear from me."

"Nah, it ain't that. It's just shit done lightweight got outta hand up here."

After giving him a brief rundown without using names, the line was silent for a minute before D-Wub replied, "I'm on my way."

Suge nodded and replied, "A'ight."

"An' don't be so hard on yo'self, Blood," D-Wub added before disconnecting the call. "Sometimes there can't be peace without a lot of sufferin' first."

***

Two days later

After Ciara finished helping her daughter, Savannah, get dressed for her small party at Chuck E. Cheese, she squatted down before the little girl and asked, "Are you sure you don't wanna wear a scarf on somethin', sweetie?"

Savannah rubbed a hand over her bald head, then bravely answered, "No, momma. I'm fine. I'ma big girl."

While only a handful of people knew about Savannah, even less knew that the six-year-old had been diagnosed with cancer nearly a year ago. Ciara had been heartbroken when she unexpectedly learned that her daughter had what doctors called an inoperable brain tumor.

She would have to undergo the painful treatments of radiation and chemotherapy. And without health insurance, unless she could personally cover the medical bills, Savannah's chances of survival became one in five.

Her parents deceased and Savannah's father doing a life sentence, Ciara singlehandedly found the strength to put down her grief and pick up her grind. While running up a check, she located a qualified specialist outside the country who said he could successfully perform the operation for $100,000.

And only death would prevent her from cashing him out. So for those who considered her unladylike, Ciara was actually just doing the best she could in trying to save her daughter's life.

"Do you know you're the most special girl in the world?" Ciara smiled down at Savannah as they were walking outside to the car.

"Yup!"

"An' do you also know how much mommy loves you?"

Savannah looked up at her mother with a serious expression. "I know you love you me a whole bunch, momma. And I love you a whole bunch, too."

Inside the car, Ciara strapped her inside her booster seat and kissed her forehead. "My little angel."

Coming around to the driver's side of her car, Ciara was reaching for her door handle when a van door slid open and a masked man jumped out. Quickly snatching her up, he placed a latex-gloved hand over her mouth to muffle her screams as she wildly bucked in his arms.

Savannah desperately tried to unbuckle her seatbelt as she fearfully witnessed the abduction.

As Ciara was forced into the van, the driver skirted out before the abductor could fully slide his door closed, leaving a six-year-old girl in the parking lot screaming for her mother.

***

Suge, Moo-Moo, and Ghost were quietly settled around a dining room table when they heard the back door open. Seconds later, D-Wub and Bella entered the room.

"Sit back down," he told them, motioning with his hand as he pulled out a chair and took a seat with Bella attentively at his side.

D-Wub fired up a 'Port before speaking. "I spent fifty racks on guns an' ammo 'cause I know going to war is sometimes necessary. Even beneficial. So when I heard about the funeral home demo' an' saw how thirty-caliber machine guns were left at the crime scene, I shrugged it off. 'Cause it was for a cause." He paused to hit the square. "Or so I thought."

Stubbing out the cigarette, he drug his chair over to Ghost and sat right in front of him. "Look me in my eyes, Blood."

Unafraid of anything, Ghost turned to face a man whose actions were unpredictable.

"This shit ain't over lil' Fred, is it?"

Knowing Bhomas' life depended on his answer, the room was intensely quiet as Ghost weighed his options. He could either tell the truth and sentence his comrade to death, or stand behind his lie and hopefully spare him. He chose the latter. "Until proven otherwise, then I can only stand behind what the homie say, 'Wub."

Nodding as if that was the answer he was expecting, D-Wub scooted his chair back and got up. After locking Bella inside the bathroom, he tied a crispy red rag around his neck, then pulled out a lemon-squeeze and held it down at his side.

"Get up, Blood," he told Ghost from across the room.

When he hesitantly complied, D-Wub continued, "Now draw yo' shit an' make sho' one in the head. Then on the count of three, we gon' cowboy the fuck up."

Ghost was reaching toward his waist when he paused to look at D-Wub with a disbelieving expression. "You willin' to *kill* me, Blood?"

"You willin' to die for what you believe is loyalty, an' I'm willin' to die for what I believe is righteousness."

"But what's so unrighteous about me backin' up a homie?"

"The homie you backin' up a *snake*. An' since you can't seem to see it, I'm thinkin' you niggas must be related."

Ghost's eyes instantly blazed with anger. "I've been loyal since day one, Blood. Flyin' my flag with the *utmost* integrity. So don't associate me wit' no snake shit." Behind his reputation, he would readily put his head on the chopping block.

Suge and Moo-Moo curiously watched as Ghost pulled out his strap and laid it on the table. Then, walking over to D-Wub, he got down on his knees and fearlessly lifted his chin. "If you really feel in yo' heart that I'm disloyal, then push my shit back right now, Blood. 'Cause I can't continue to follow a man that don't trust me."

After holding his stare for what seemed like an eternity, D-Wub extended his hand and pulled Ghost up from the floor. "I luh you, Blood," he said from the heart as they shook up and hugged.

D-Wub let Bella out the bathroom and called everyone into the living room, where he fed a disc into a DVD player and pressed play. An image of Ciara noisily slurping on Jinx appeared on the TV screen. This was a scene from the movie he had secretly recorded that night at the Hawthorne titled *Ratchet Hoez Exposed.*

"This what that clown ass nigga Bhomas got us goin' to war over," D-Wub said in disgust as he pointed at the screen. "He been lying 'bout gettin' into it wit' them Crip niggas the whole time. This shit all over some *pussy.* Pussy that ain't even his. An' the nigga's treachery don't end there." He paused to fire up a square. "He the one that robbed Suge."

As Moo-Moo and Ghost looked at him in disbelief, he continued, "Think about it. These niggas done already put two of ours in *body bags.* So don't you think if it was really them that caught Suge slippin' like that, they woulda drilled 'im for the stripes? Them niggas ain't sparin' no known member of the 'Pack."

Suge then cut in to explain how Turk's baby momma had worriedly called him and said that he never made it home the other night. "My intuition say Blood stumbled across evidence of this niggas treachery, an' Bhomas made sho' he ain't here to speak on it."

While D-Wub was explaining how they would move from here, Ghost was still thinking about everything he had just learned. He couldn't believe how loyal he had been to a man who was clearly only out for himself. It made him wonder what was truly in the hearts of everyone present.

"What's on yo' mind?" D-Wub asked him as they were leaving the house.

"I woulda died for this nigga, Blood," Ghost answered with an hurt expression. "An' he lied to me. Had me on the front line for some bullshit."

D-Wub nodded in understanding, then offered the only advice he felt would suit the occasion. "Then make sho' it's a closed casket."

As Ghost and Moo-Moo slid off in the same car, Suge approached D-Wub as he was climbing inside the Hellcat. "As a favor to me, I'm askin' that you spare Ciara. This wasn't her fault, gotti."

Neicy had called him last night on some hysterical shit, explaining how Ciara had been kidnapped right in front of her daughter's eyes. "You know my girl's situation, Suge. So if there's anything you can do, I'm askin' you to please do it." Suge was indeed one of the few who knew about Savannah, as well as the reason behind Ciara's relentless pursuit of money.

D-Wub brought the Hemi to life, then looked up at him and replied, "Too much blood done been spilt over this bitch, Suge. She *can't* live."

Kweli

Chapter 19

When Ghost pulled up to Moo-Moo's crib, he turned to his comrade with genuine concern. "Wassup wit' that situation in there?" he asked as he nudged his head toward the house.

"It's cool," Moo-Moo answered, staring out the passenger window. "I'ma just give her what she want an' get lil' bra up outta there."

"You know what need to happen," Ghost countered in disagreement. "An' I'm sayin', just gimme the word."

Moo-Moo made direct eye contact with him before replying, "I can't do that to my own momma, gotti. So just let me take care of it."

"A'ight, Blood," Ghost said and shrugged. "It's yo' call."

After watching Moo-Moo disappear inside the house, Ghost slowly pulled away from the curb, not knowing this was the last time they would ever see each other.

***

Bound and gagged inside a small trunk, Ciara could feel every bump in the road as she was being driven to who knows where. After crying until there were no more tears, she was now praying to a God she had never believed in.

"Please protect my baby, Lord. Don't let my actions deprive her of your mercy. I won't make no excuses for myself, but I didn't know no other way to save her life."

Ciara was so deep into her prayer, she was unaware of the car stopping until she heard the trunk open. She wiggled and loudly groaned in fear while being lifted out.

"Stop movin', bitch!" an unfamiliar voice barked as he cut the zip ties from her ankles. She felt a glimpse of hope when he freed her hands. *Lord, I promise to be a better person.*

When the blindfold was removed, that bit of hope quickly vanished as she looked from the merciless eyes of D-Wub to the heavily-wooded area of Pearson Park.

"Wub, I—"

He held up a hand to silence her. "Don't talk, just listen." Accompanied by Boss and Smoke, who had assisted in the kidnapping, they had no idea as to what his intentions were.

"To prove I'm not the monster you think I am," D-Wub continued, "I'ma give you a chance to live. You get a sixty-second headstart, an' if you can make it to the other side of the park without gettin' caught, then you free. Simple as that."

Ciara looked toward the pitch black forest, then back at D-Wub. "Sixty seconds?" She knew there was a 7-Eleven on the other side.

He held up his right hand. "Sixty full seconds."

After Boss was asked to keep the time, the silent assassin eyed his watch until the second hand neared the twelve, then told Ciara to run.

As she took off into the woods at full speed, D-Wub casually spun toward the car and opened the back door, allowing Bella to jump out. Boss and Smoke exchanged a curious look when he pulled out a green apple and caused the dog to immediately go into a seated position.

"Time?"

Boss glanced at his watch. "Fifty seconds."

D-Wub pocketed the apple, then opened his other hand, which held a torn piece of Ciara's clothing, and put it up to Bella's nose. When he was certain she had the scent, he commanded, "*Kill!*" Then proudly watched as she instantly took off in Ciara's direction.

He was halfway through a cigarette when they heard the first of several piercing screams echo from deep inside the woods.

Minutes later, Bella came trotting back toward them with blood all over her mouth. She took a seat before D-Wub, then licked her bloody chops once while eagerly eyeing his pocket.

Nah, that definitely ain't no show dog, Smoke thought to himself as he watched D-Wub feed her the apple.

***

During the same time Ghost was being pulled over and arrested for carrying a concealed weapon, Moo-Moo was fighting for his life. He had just finished checking on his brother Boogie when he bumped into Eddie outside in the hallway.

"What's poppin', nigga?" he barked as the guerrilla-sized junkie purposely blocked his path.

"Let me hold a couple grams," Eddie replied with a wicked gleam in his eyes. "An' you can deduct it from what you owe."

His consent coming too fast, Moo-Moo nodded and said, "A'ight, I got you." Then underestimated Eddie for a second time by turning his back on him.

Knowing Moo-Moo would return with a gun instead, Eddie quickly put him in a chokehold and literally lifted him off his feet. "You shoulda used it the first time," he whispered to Moo-Moo as he carried him to his room. "Now I'ma teach yo' bitch ass 'bout pullin' out a gun an' not usin' it."

Moo-Moo desperately clawed at Eddie's face as he felt himself going to sleep. Not knowing if he would ever awaken, he was now wishing he had listened to Ghost.

Who gon' look out for Boogie? was his last thought before losing consciousness.

"Yeah, nigga," Eddie teased as he continued to squeeze. "Go night-night." After squeezing for a minute longer, he carelessly let Moo-Moo's body collapse to the floor, then ransacked the room until he found an ounce of heroin hidden inside the closet. Instantly consumed with greed, he dumped several grams into a sandwich bag and tucked the rest inside his underwear.

Charlene was standing at the bottom of the staircase as Eddie came down. "What the hell was all that noise up there?"

He held up the sandwich bag and dangled it, "You wanna ask a bunch of questions or you wanna get that *monkey* off yo' back?"

Her gaze going from the top of the staircase over to Eddie as he anxiously tied a rubber string around his arm, Charlene shamefully hurried over to the couch. She would later learn that Moo-Moo's

130

death was not instant and that he could have been revived had she chosen him over her addiction.

***

While Ciara's gruesome death was being broadcasted over every news channel in Toledo, D-Wub and his southern soldiers were already back in the 'Nati tearing down the mall.

Later that night, they were going to a club in Mt. Healthy called The Ave, where Smoke and Pistol would open up for Moneybagg Yo. With elite from all over the city guaranteed to be in attendance, D-Wub would ensure it was a night to remember.

Kweli

Chapter 20

Suge was in the middle of serving four and a half to an older cat from the north, when he got a 911 text from Neicy. This being unusual, he hit her up as soon as he hopped back inside his Challenger.

"What up?" he asked in concern when she answered.

"I can't do it no more, Suge."

"Can't do what?"

"None of this shit," she replied in a distressed tone. "It's too much killin' goin' on in this little ass city an' I gotta go."

"Neicy—"

"I already bought a bus ticket to New York that leaves tonight, so I'm just telling you so you can get yo' stuff."

"Listen to me, Neicy. I already know you fucked behind yo' girl, but don't make no decision without first thinking it through." He glanced at his watch. "Look, I gotta few more stops to make, then I'm headed yo' way."

"Suge, ain't nothing you say gon' make me wanna continue to stay here. It's time for me to move on."

"I understand all that. But I'm saying, at least let me see you before you dip. Damn, a nigga aint worthy of that?"

The line was silent for a minute before Neicy replied, "My bus leaves at ten. So if you here before then, we'll talk. If not, I'll see you when I see you."

***

As J-Bo was escorted into a small room used for attorney visits, Wingate waited until the deputy closed the door before reaching out for a firm handshake.

"Jovante," he greeted with a genuine smile.

"What's good, Phil?" J-Bo replied with the same energy.

"Just doin' a temperature check."

Since becoming his lawyer, Wingate would stop by the county at least once a week, even if it was only for a few minutes of miscellaneous convo. He was simply giving J-Bo what he would want given to him if roles were reversed, constant reassurance. Something Wingate knew went a long way with a man facing the death penalty.

As they were wrapping up their visit, Wingate casually informed him of Ciara's death. "They say it was some type of vicious animal attack."

J-Bo just nodded in response, thinking to himself, *Karma a mu'fucka.*

Once he was back inside his kennel, J-Bo waited for the C.O. to do his round, then used a blanket to block the airway at the bottom of his door. Grabbing two staples and a set of AA batteries, he then took out the gram of weed Wingate had slipped him during their initial handshake and rolled it up in a piece of Bible paper. Being the closest thing to a zigzag, this was a common practice among prisoners all over the world.

After blowing the pinky-size joint, J-Bo listened to his walkman as he laid in his rack and enjoyed the high. His mind roamed everywhere before settling on Juan-Juan, as usual. He knew his mans was out there somewhere watching over him.

I miss you, my nigga, he thought to himself, then suddenly recalled an incident that made him laugh out loud.

***

Camped out down the street from a weed house that did numbers, Juan-Juan and J-Bo sat low in a mercury with MAC-1's beneath their trench coats. In the early morning hours of a Friday, they were patiently waiting for the routine drop of fifteen pounds of gas.

Their palms began to sweat inside the latex when a charger pulled up to the house and two men ran outside to meeti it. One clutching a 30-round pole while animatedly looking around, the other grabbed a trash bag out of the trunk and they hurried back inside the house as the car sped off.

"We know it's at least four of 'em in there," J-Bo reasoned as he pulled the Mercury around the corner. "So we' gon' have to hit this bitch like S.W.A.T."

This being music to Juan-Juan's ears, he wordlessly chambered one in the MAC's head and rolled the ski mask down over his face. As they crept to the back of the house, J-Bo held up his fist, counted to three, then booted the door in.

Juan-Juan soldiered into the house and quickly crushed the first three as one raising a 30-round glock. The fourth vic' fired several wild shots as he ran upstairs. Juan-Juan's murder game on ma-

rine-level, he exchanged the MAC for a Desert and went to go hunt him down.

As J-Bo heard the cannon barking upstairs, he found the pounds inside a leather couch. Quickly bagging them up, he slung the duffel over his shoulder and impatiently looked toward the staircase. "Fuck this nigga doin'?" he fumed to himself as he cautiously made his way up.

When J-Bo peered into a bedroom and saw Juan-Juan frozen in place, he followed his eyes, which were intently staring at the floor. Juan-Juan being terrified of snakes, there was baby python lying between him and the doorway. J-Bo thoughtlessly bent down to grab the snake and threw it under the bed. "Come on, fam. Jet's roll."

Once they were a safe distance away from the crime scene, J-Bo suddenly busted out laughing as he braked at a red light. Juan-Juan shot him an unamused glare.

"Don't worry, my nigga, " J-Bo assured him as he continued to laugh. "I won't tell nobody yo' vicious killin'ass was scared of a lil' garden snake."

***

9:26 p.m.

As Suge sped up to Neicy's crib with a bottle of Ciroc and a bag of Chinese food, his plan was to get her tipsy. Then viciously dick her down until she was too exhausted to leave before he ate the shrimp-fried rice while watching highlights on ESPN.

While he may not have been ready for a committed relationship, Neicy had became an asset he was not willing to let go of. Having passed several of his bait tests, she had proved to be a trustworthy woman whose survival was not based on handouts.

Using his key to get inside, Suge saw her luggage in the living room and immediately knew two things. She wasn't gone yet, but was dead serious about leaving.

"Aye, Neicy!" he called out as he took the stairs two at a time.

"Yeah!" she answered from inside her bedroom. Bent over in gray leggings, she was rummaging through one of her dresser drawers.

Smiling as he stepped through the doorway, Suge's expression instantly changed as the barrel of a 12-Gauge was put to his temple.

"On *Geer,* I'll blow yo' shit off!" Shooter promised as he held the gauge in steady hands.

With a reptilian coldness in his eyes, Blueface stepped from behind the bedroom door clutching a chrome 500-Revolver. He sized Suge up, then buckled him with a hook to his stomach. "Take some of that air out yo' chest, Cuzz."

As Shooter nudged his head for Neicy to leave the room, Suge looked up at her with a look of disbelief. "Fa real?"

Eying him in hatred, she replied, "I could've got over you usin' me, 'cause that's all you were doin'. But you crossed the line when you killed my girl. Especially after I personally explained her situation to you." Neicy then laid a hand over her stomach and added, "So the same way Savannah will have to grow up without her mother is the same way yo' child will have to grow up without its father." Recently finding out she was six weeks pregnant, Neicy had never got the chance to tell him he would soon be a father.

Before Suge could offer any type of reaction, Shooter put him to sleep with the butt of the gauge.

After throwing her luggage into the back of her Chrysler Pacifica, Neicy walked over to a 2014 Suburban and climbed into its backseat. Up front, Jinx sat behind the wheel while Fat-Cat rode shotgun.

"That bag on the other seat is yours," Fat-Cat said as he slightly turned in her direction. "Consider it a token of my appreciation." Inside the small bag was $25,000.

Neicy briefly eyed it before replying with a head shake, "I'm good, 'Cat. I didn't do what I did out of thirst. I did it out of loyalty to my girl." Not knowing that Suge had tried to prevent Ciara's death, Neicy held him responsible. And rather than seek criminal justice from authorities, she would let the streets be his judge, jury, and executioner.

As Neicy was about to pull off in the Pacifica, Jinx tapped on her window. When she lowered it halfway, he stuck the bag through the opening and dropped it on her lap. "You might not want it, but you definitely gon' need it."

While on the turnpike headed to New York, Neicy glanced at her passenger with affection and said, "I love you."

Savannah looked at her and smiled, "I love you, too, Auntie Neicy."

When Ciara was being kidnapped, she had managed to reach inside her purse and purposely drop her phone. In her being thoroughly prepared, she had taught Savannah how to use it. She specifically instructed her to call Neicy in the event of an emergency.

"If anything ever happens to me, I want you to call Auntie Neicy an' no one else, Ok?"

"Ok, momma," she had obediently answered.

As Neicy reached over to hold one of Savannah's hands, she was simply upholding the promise she had made to Ciara the day she had called her from Applebee's. That was to look after her daughter as if she were own.

Kweli

Chapter 21

Cincinnati

Inside their recently bought studio, courtesy of D-Wub, Pistol and Smoke were in the booth laying a track to a Metro Boomin-like beat. Turned up and shirtless, they were rehearsing their verses with the same energy as they would later that night at the club.

In hoodies and Timbs, Joe-Joe and Boss arrived just as they were finishing the song.

"Blood, you gotta hear this shit!" Pistol excitedly told Boss as he came out the booth and shook up with him and Joe-Joe.

Heads bobbed in unison as the engineer played the song back. It was definitely a club banger.

As soon as the engineer packed up his laptop and left, Smoke turned toward Pistol and punched him in the mouth, knocking out two of his fronts.

The unexpected blow put Pistol on his back. "What the fuck!?" he cried out in fear and confusion as he held a hand over his bleeding mouth.

"Not only did you apologize, but you shook my *hand*," Joe-Joe growled as he stood over Pistol with a look of disgust. "I specifically told you D-Wub a nigga I'm willin' to die fo', but you *still* turnt right around an' tried to convince Smoke to indulge in yo' fuckery. Nigga, you worse than the opps. At least wit' them, I know what to expect."

Boss stepped around Joe-Joe and motioned for Pistol to get up. "Come on, bra. Let me get you up outta here."

As he nervously rose to his feet, Boss put a hand on his shoulder reassuringly. Magically, he produced a Bowie knife in his other hand and savagely drove it into his cousin's stomach.

Pistol's eyes bulged as he loudly gasped in shock.

When Pistol had revealed his heart to Smoke that day, with there being no gray area in Smoke's loyalty, he knew he had no choice but to expose Pistol for who he was.

After informing Joe-Joe, who in turn notified Boss, they unanimously decided that Pistol had to be put down. To remove him from their circle and let him live would be too risky.

"I'll do it," Boss had quietly volunteered from the backseat. With Pistol being his first cousin, Joe-Joe and Smoke both shot him a questioning look, to which he replied, "Blood makes us related, but loyalty makes us family."

Unable to speak, Pistol could only stare at Boss in disbelief as he felt the knife twisting on his insides. Never in a million years would he have imagined he would die at the hands of his own cousin. The same man who had introduced him to the game. The same man he had taken baths with as a child.

There was no sympathy in Boss' stare as he watched the life slowly drain from Pistol's eyes. Before pulling the knife out, he leaned near his ear and whispered, "Sometimes lessons not learned in blood are soon forgotten. Rest in peace, cuz."

***

Later that night

As a mile-long line of people stood outside The Ave waiting to get in, they heard the Humvee from a block away. When it rolled into the parking lot a minute later on 32-inch Forgis, the bass from inside the crimson-colored H-1, sent vibrations through everyone in line while setting off multiple car alarms.

All four doors pushed open and D-Wub, Joe-Joe, Boss, and Smoke hopped out the tank in fatigues and unlaced Wheaties. A Camaro around their neck and a Charger on their wrists, Joe-Joe led the way with a Prada bag slung over his shoulder.

As they bypassed the line and were escorted to their elevated booth in V.I.P., natives of the city were curious as to who D-Wub was. But the coldness in his eyes discouraged them from openly staring.

Within minutes, their booth was full of bad bitches and buckets of champagne. A gumbo thick red-bone in a mini dress sat next to D-Wub. "I'm Angel," she introduced herself with a flirtatious smile.

Displaying self-control, his expression remained stoic as he told her his name.

"So, where you from, D-Wub?" Angel continued as she approvingly eyed his VVS-flooded chain and bejeweled earlobe. "'Cause I've never seen you around here before."

He was on the verge of answering, when he and a woman down on the dance floor locked eyes. Rocking a denim jacket over a midriff T-shirt that exposed her toned stomach, she was standing pigeon-toed. She wore a pair of Missoni sandals with Polo jeans straining over her voluptuous thighs. Her skin tone the color of almonds, she would intimidate the average man.

Excusing himself from the table, D-Wub boldly breezed down on her as she stood with a group of equally attractive women. "I'm D-Wub," he said, extending his hand.

She offered him hers and smiled, "I'm September."

Still holding her manicured hand, he invited her and her friends up to his booth. "It's enough bottles for everybody." Her bubble jiggling through the jeans, D-Wub could only shake his head in lust as he followed her up the short flight of stairs.

When it was time for Smoke to take the stage, he did two fire-ass solos before telling Joe-Joe, Boss, and D-Wub to join him. Then, as he performed the club banger he and Pistol had made in the studio that day, they pulled out five racks apiece, while standing at the edge of the stage and made it rain.

As the crowd went nuts, three young hitters from Winton Terrace were in the cut enviously eyeing the stage; their gazes locked on D-Wub. Common sense told them he was the reason behind Joe-Joe and his team's overnight success.

"Leave this bitch early," one of the killers spoke into another's ear. "We going home wit' buddy tonight."

At the end of his performance, Smoke thanked the city for their love and support, then made an announcement that would definitely make it a memorable night. "Every drink in this bitch on us!"

Regarded as hood celebrities as they walked back to their booth, September now knew with a certainty she was in the presence of a boss. And the chemistry between her and D-Wub was undeniable.

After Moneybagg did his thing and the club was letting out, D-Wub told September he was riding with her and to tell her friends goodnight.

Loving a man who took charge, she replied, "Yes sir, Mr. 'Wub."

Joe-Joe was coming from an office in the back where he'd just paid the $40,000 liquor tab, when he bumped into a young savage he knew named Shake-D', short for Shakedown. And not only did he recognize a predatory look in his eyes, but he noticed that D-Wub was only a few people ahead.

As he and Shake-D shook up, Joe-Joe leaned near his ear and said, "That shit *dead*, Blood."

An intense stare off occurred before Shake-D reluctantly stood down. "A'ight, Joe-Joe." He yielded with a head nod. "I'ma respect yo' wishes."

"Ain't no *wishes*," Joe-Joe corrected. "It's a *warnin'*."

As Shake-D heatedly watched him step off, he sent his men outside a quick text, but made a silent vow that this was far from over. *Now I'm at yo' neck too bitch ass nigga.*

***

The Radisson Hotel

Already naked, September was lightweight disappointed as she laid in the bed watching D-Wub undress. While his chiselled frame was decorated in ink from ears to ankles, his dick size measured short of her standard 8-inch rule. *I shoulda knew this nigga was too good to be true.*

Confidently stepping over to the bed, D-Wub grabbed her by the ankles and snatched her to its edge. He trailed gentle kisses from her feet to her inner thighs, then licked everywhere but on the pretty lips of her bald box. His tongue game official, it wasn't long before she was loudly begging for him to drink out of her faucet.

As tempting as it may have been, eating strange pussy on the first night was forbidden. So, flipping her over instead, he carried her quivering body to center of the bed and slid into her with the intent to prove that experience outweighed size.

After her third record-breaking orgasm, September tried to crawl away as his hips continued to swing in a way that enabled him to reach   every crevice of her insides. The feeling of disappointment now one of amazement, she couldn't believe he was pleasuring her better than men nearly twice his length.

Determined to engrave his name in her memory, D-Wub balled her up and did hula-hoops, pushups, and squats inside the pussy for thirty nonstop minutes. It wasn't until her sweat-soaked body went limp from exhaustion, did he snatch off the rubber and skeet all over her fat ass.

Wearing a smirk of amusement as he stared down at her well-fucked expression, D-Wub fired up a square while thinking to himself, *Yeah, I know you doubted me, bitch.*

***

Meanwhile

Suge was instantly stricken with fear as he regained consciousness. Spread eagle with a strip of duct tape over his mouth, he was tied down to Neicy's kitchen table. Lifting his head in panic, he saw Jinx, Blueface, and Shooter patiently standing before him blowing a blunt of pressure.

"You can make this shit painless or painful, Cuzz," Jinx informed him in between tokes. "It's up to you. All we wanna know is where D-Wub an' nem at."

Suge uselessly struggled against the rope as Blueface and Shooter approached the table from either side. When Blueface snatched off the tape, Suge spit at him and hissed, "Eat a *dick*, crab ass nigga!"

Blueface grinned as he took off shirt. "You talkin' that shit right now, but you definitely gon' break."

As Shooter threw a towel over Suge's face and held his head in place, Blueface grabbed a bucket of water from under the table and began pouring it over him. Known as water boarding, this was an horrific form of torture that had been banned by the U.N.

Desperately gasping for air, Suge was struggling to breathe as water went inside his mouth and nose. It literally felt like he was drowning. Needless to say, he broke down after several buckets. He even told them about the five bricks in the basement.

"You coulda did this the first time," Blueface said in irritation as he drew the 500-Revolver and fired twice.

Boom! Boom!

Chapter 22

Charlene was on her way inside the house when Blueface crept up behind her and placed his hand over her mouth. "Scream an' I'm killin' you," he warned, while pressing a gun into her ribs. "Now unlock the fuckin' doe."

As they entered the darkened house, Cam and Duke rushed in behind him and went to look for Moo-Moo.

Wrinkling his nose at a vicious stench inside the house, Blueface looked at Charlene and asked, "Fuck is that *smell*?"

Before she could answer, Duke came back downstairs in a hurry. "Aye, Cuzz. We gotta roll."

"Why, wassup?"

"The nigga already dead."

Blueface frowned. "He already dead?"

"Yeah, Cuzz," Duke nodded.

"You *sho*?"

"Cuzz, I aint gotta check a nigga pulse to know he gone." He nudged his head toward the stairs. "But he up there in a closet if you wanna see for yo'self."

Cam then came back into the front room wearing a sickened expression. He glared at Charlene and slowly shook his head. "You a foul ass bitch." He went on to explain how he found a little boy chained up in the basement with a bowl of water and no food. "The lil' nigga layin' in his own shit an' piss."

Kweli

With no choice but to tuck his emotions, Blueface told Charlene to lie facedown on the couch and count to sixty.

They were walking to the front door when Cam felt a movement behind him and smoothly pivoted with his gun extended. "What the fuck we tell you?" he spazzed on Charlene as she came toward them. Scratching her body the way heroin addicts often did when in need, she pleaded, "Baby, I'm sick. If you could just throw me a tenth, I would be so grateful." She reached one of her ashy hands toward his crotch and added, "I can earn it if you want me to."

Cam smacked her hand away in disgust and pressed the barrel into her forehead. "Bitch, don't *ever* put yo' fucking hands on me!"

"It's cool, Cuzz," Blueface said as he laid a calming hand on Cam's shoulder. "She lost right now."

Pulling out a small bankroll, Blueface balled up a huncho and tossed it at her. "Get that lil' nigga from outta that basement an' get 'im something to eat. 'Cause if I come back an' see otherwise, you gon' be more than sick."

They slid through Ghost spot next. But luckily for him, he was still in the county waiting for Suge to post his $50,000 bond. Clueless as to what was taking place in the streets, he would learn of the casualties through the local news.

***

With his arm in a sling, Bhomas was laying on the couch watching *Menace to Society* when the front door was kicked in and three masked men blitzed his crib. Before he could reach for his strap, Shooter viciously cracked him with the butt of a gun, then motioned for Eli and Pig to search the house.

Pig returned a minute later with Bhomas' younger brother, who had his hands up in surrender.

"I found Cuzz hidin' under the bed," Pig proudly announced. Eager to earn some stars and bars, the sixteen-year-old had literally begged Shooter to bring him along.

Eli was nervously looking around upstairs when he heard a faint noise come from inside the bathroom. Slowly opening the door, he peeked behind it, then eased toward the tub and snatched back its shower curtain.

Her body trembling in fear, Bhomas' elderly grandmother was crouched down inside the tub holding a pair of scissors.

While Shooter's instructions had been to kill anything breathing, Eli didn't have the heart to squeeze. Placing a finger to his lips, he quietly closed the door and went back downstairs.

"Wasn't nobody up there," he told Shooter in his most convincing tone.

"You checked everywhere?"

"On Geer, Cuzz."

Shooter told him to go get the car ready, then turned back to Bhomas as he and his brother were lying facedown on the carpeted floor. He took off his mask and made Bhomas roll over.

"Look like it's gon' be yo' face on back of a sweater now," he said before he bit his bottom lip and fired all facials.

Boc! Boc! Boc! Boc!

Unaffected by the crocodile tears Bhomas' brother was now shedding, Shooter gave Pig the greenlight on his first kill. "Gone an' get one under yo' belt, Loc."

As Eli sat behind the wheel constantly checking the rearview, he flinched when three more shots rang out inside the house.

Damn, I hope that nigga aint go upstairs, he thought to himself, while looking toward the house and slowly shaking his head.

It had taken for this gang war to happen for Eli to finally accept that he was involved in a lifestyle he wasn't built for. But because he was buried so deeply within it, he knew death would most likely be his only means of escape.

***

The following afternoon

Three cars deep, in two Escalades and a Hellcat, Shooter and a football team of Crips were taking a field trip down to the 'Nati. There they would officially end the war by knocking off the head of the Wolf Pack, D-Wub. With a licensed driver behind the wheel of each car, they were travelling with automatic weapons and murderous mindsets.

They arrived in the 'Nati three hours later and got off on the Vine and Mitchell exit. After passing a number of gas stations and restaurants, they came around a bend and saw a sign that read, "Welcome to Winton Terrace."

Blueface called Shooter from the rear S.U.V. and alerted him of the Terrace's treacherous reputation, which he had heard about in D.Y.S.

"They say these niggas' savages, Cuzz. So we definitely gon' have to be on point."

A large crowd of people were standing outside the neighborhood store on Kingsrun when the three-car motorcade entered the parking lot, he Hellcat leading the way. Their movements elegant from experience, several active assassins among the crowd were clutching semi's within seconds.

All eyes were on Shooter as he unfolded himself from the passenger seat of the 'Lac truck and boldly soldiered toward the store's entrance. As his un-blinking eyes met hardened stares along the way, the noticeable bulge beneath his blue hoodie indicated he was packing at least 30-rounds.

After buying a pack of swishers and asking the store clerk for directions to Price Hill, Shooter stepped back outside and purposely locked eyes with a fellow savage.

"What's craccin', homie?"

The young savage simply lifted his head in acknowledgement.

"I'm lookin' for a nigga named D-Wub from Toledo, Cuzz. Light skin nigga wit' a Mohawk. Be wit' Joe-Joe outta Price Hill."

Shake-D shook his head and lied with a straight face, "Never heard of 'im."

Shooter nodded, "A'ight, Cuzz." Then two-finger saluted before turning to walk off.

As he watched Shooter climb back inside the Escalade, Shake-D knew his chances of taking D-Wub up top had just greatly decreased. Because niggas didn't venture into foreign territory and blatantly look for a man unless they were ready to spill blood.

These niggas 'bout to fuck my lick up, he fumed to himself as the three cars exited the parking lot in unison.

***

Joe-Joe was standing on the back porch clutching an MP5 when D-Wub pulled the Denali up to the back of the house. With him and his hounds now handing out more work than a temp service, D-Wub had to shoot to his storage unit and pick up four more bricks.

Grabbing a small bag from under the seat, D-Wub hopped out the truck and left his door open. From here, he was on his way to meet September at Dave and Busters.

Dutifully riding shotgun, Bella's coal-black eyes followed him every step of the way. And as D-Wub was on the verge of handing Joe-Joe the bag, she peeped a masked-up man ducked down on side of the house, creeping. Her loyalty unquestionable, Bella immediately leaped out through the driver side door and raced in his direction, which is what would save D-Wub's life.

The gunman was a split second from squeezing when he saw Bella charging at him. Throwing his arm just as she lunged for his neck, he cried out when her powerful jaws locked on his forearm.

"Aaahhhh!"

Doom! Doom! Doom! Doom!

Reacting without hesitation at the sound of the gunshots, Joe-Joe grabbed D-Wub and pushed him into the house while squeezing three-round bursts in the unseen gunman's direction.

Bdddd! Bddddd! Bddddd!

As Joe-Joe was backing into the house, another shooter came from behind the Denali with a modified AR-15.

Tat! Tat! Tat! Tat! Tat! Tat! Tat! Tat! Tat!

D-Wub and Joe-Joe scrambled to the living room, where D-Wub grabbed a fully-auto Mac from under the couch.

Outside, four ski-mask-wearing commandos stood side-by-side, squeezing finger-size slugs into the house.

The barrage of bullets barely missing them, D-Wub and Joe-Joe knew they had to get on offense if they wanted to stay alive. So, without a word spoken, Joe-Joe stuck the MP5 around the corner and let off a whole cartridge. Then, while reloading, D-Wub squeezed thirty-two shots from the Mac. They repeated this cycle for a minute straight, spitting out hundreds of rounds.

As the squad outside was now forced to play defense, the lead soldier signalled for his men to retreat. The hit had been foiled and the police would be on scene at any minute. Quickly dispersing, they jumped back in the Hellcat and skirted out.

After the fireworks ended, D-Wub cautiously crept out the back door with the Mac extended. Peeking around the side of the house, his heart broke when he saw Bella lying motionless on the ground.

"Bella!" he called out as he ran over to her and got down on one knee.

Her body riddled with bullet holes, she had somehow managed to cling to life long enough to see D-Wub one last time.

As their eyes met, a single tear rolled down his cheek.

"Aye, 'Wub," Joe-Joe interrupted in a gentle tone. "We gotta go, Blood."

D-Wub nodded while continuing to stare into Bella's dying eyes. "I love you, girl," he said before ending her misery with one in the skull.

Chapter 23

The Next Day

After the unsuccessful attempt on D-Wub's life, which a heroin-addict had made possible for three grams, Shooter and his men had to get on the road and disappointedly head back to the city. Because they could've never predicted a dog would act as D-Wub's savior, the war would continue.

Blueface, who had been the one bitten by Bella, had to be dropped off at the emergency room where he learned he would have to undergo surgery for the torn ligaments in his forearm. So, while he may have killed Bella, he would bear a vicious scar that would always remind him of his encounter with the Land Shark.

At Eli's crib, he and Shooter were blowing kush and wiping down shells when Keedra tiredly came home from work.

"Eli, what I tell you 'bout smokin' that shit up in here!?" she snapped as she protectively placed a hand over her five month pregnant stomach. "An' why you bringin' the streets home wit' you anyway where we lay our head at?"

Keedra angrily turned and stomped upstairs, mumbling along the way. "Sometimes I swear this nigga be actin' like a goofy."

"Aye, let me holla at this bitch real quick," Eli told Shooter as he stubbed the blunt out. "I'll be right back."

Kweli

He came back downstairs thirty minutes later looking troubled. "Come on, Cuzz. Let's roll. This bitch trippin'."

After a quiet ride to Shooter's apartment, they hid the small arsenal in the mattress, then twisted another blunt and played Call of Duty.

Shooter paused the game in the middle of a mission and turned to Eli. "I think it's time for you to get out these trenches, Cuzz."

Eli frowned in confusion. "What you mean?"

"I'm sayin', homie. I know yo' heart ain't in this shit for real. So just gone an' fall back. Yo' girl pregnant wit' yo' first child, anyway."

He took in Eli's saddened expression and continued, "We still gone be niggas, Cuzz. Ain't nothin' ever gone change that. It just ain't no reason for you to keep riskin' yo' life for somethin' you really don't even believe in. You feel me?"

His head down, Eli slowly nodded.

Crash!

The Task Force breached the front door and rolled a Flash Bang into the living room.

Bang!

"Don't move! Don't move!" a throng of voices yelled as faceless men in all black swarmed the small apartment clutching tactical weapons.

Their ears ringing and eyesight temporarily loss, Eli and Shooter were too disoriented to move as they were thrown onto the floor and cuffed. After an officer came from the back and yelled ''Clear!'', they were taken outside to a paddy wagon and transported downtown.

"Regardless of what the charges is," Shooter whispered to Eli along the way, "I'ma make sho' you out to see the birth of yo' firstborn."

He had been looking out for his friend since day one and would continue to do so until no longer able.

***

"You give us Christopher Anderson, AKA Fat-Cat, and I'll personally see to it that you're able to go to the parole board one day," Detective Cavanaugh told Shooter as he sat across from him in the interrogation room. "Because otherwise, you're looking at spending the rest of your natural life inside a maximum-security prison."

Wearing a blank expression, Shooter replied, "Can I piss now?"

"Mr. Hunter, I don't believe you understand the seriousness of your situation here. We have concrete evidence connecting you to *six murders*."

"I understand everything you sayin', officer. But like I been tellin' you for the last hour, I gotta *piss*." Shooter then looked up at the camera mounted in the corner and said, "They violatin' my rights by refusin' to let me use the bathroom."

Cavanaugh smirked as he got up to leave. He returned a minute later and told Shooter he would personally escort him to the bathroom. Cuffing his hands in front, he grabbed his arm and led him out into the hallway, where Shooter saw something that made his heart drop.

His wrists free of handcuffs, Eli was leaving the police station in a hurry.

"Elijah!" Shooter called out.

He froze in his tracks, then reluctantly turned to face a man who would've done anything for him. Eli had turned traitor the day Homicide got killed and Gang Task Force showed up at his hospital room. Already on three years probation, the detectives had his P.O. come up to the hospital and threaten to violate him for being in the company of a known gang member. "I understand your friend is dead, Mr. Turnbow, but unless you agree to cooperate with these gentlemen, then you'll leave me no choice but to send you away for the remaining two and a half years you have left on papers."

Contemplating the nightmares of prison, a jungle in which he feared he could not physically survive, along with the likelihood that his girl would lay with another man, Eli shamefully agreed to get Shooter off the streets. When he'd allegedly been upstairs talking to his girl, he had really been on the phone with Detective Cavanaugh, telling him they were on there way to Shooter's crib.

Unable to look Shooter in his eyes, Eli lowered his head and quietly apologized. "I'm sorry, Cuzz."

Though deeply hurt, Shooter smirked, "Don't worry 'bout it, bra. It's my fault. I been knew you was a coward."

Chapter 24

As D-Wub and his men were mounting up, he got a call from an unknown number. While he usually ignored such calls, his instincts made him answer.

"This is a collect call from, Ghost, an inmate in the Lucas County Corrections. To accept this call press zero, to re—"

"What's poppin', Blood?" D-Wub greeted in concern.

"What's good, big homie?"

"Fuck goin' on up there?" he questioned, speaking in reference to Ghost's situation and not being able to reach Suge.

"I'm assumin' you ain't heard."

"Heard what?"

"Suge gone, 'Wub. The nigga Bhomas, too. Moo-Moo shit goin' straight to voicemail, so I can't speak for him. Only reason I'm safe is 'cause I got pulled over an' arrested the other night for a strap."

Taking the phone away from his ear, D-Wub took a deep breath and loudly exhaled. He was blaming himself for Suge's death. He had told his men to lay low until he returned to the city, when he should've crushed Fat-Cat and his men off the *muscle*. Now he understood how the opps knew where to find him.

They must've tortured my nigga, he thought sadly to himself.

He put the phone back to his ear and told Ghost he was coming to bond him out. "An' have yo' cleats on, Blood. We straight to the field."

***

Kiona was stepping out the shower when her nude frame froze in fear. There was a masked gunman calmly standing inside her bathroom.

"Cover yo'self up," Boss said as he pointed the gun at her bath towel.

When she tried to run, he stuck his foot out and tripped her. "Please don't mistake my calmness for cowardice," he icily forewarned. "Now put the fuckin' towel on."

After complying, Boss ushered her into the adjoining bedroom and pushed her toward her phone. "Unlock it."

"I can't," Kiona lied. "It ain't mine."

Boss put her to sleep with the butt of his gun, then used her right thumb to unlock the phone. He found Fat-Cat's number listed under "Hubby" and sent him a brief text that read, *"Somebody broke into the house, Fat-Cat. I'm scared."*

Turning off the phone, he quickly tied her up and went back downstairs where Smoke was occasionally peeking out the window. "Let's roll, Blood."

As they climbed back inside a tinted Durango, Boss looked over his shoulder and said, "It's done."

D-Wub and Ghost did a weapons check, then wordlessly hopped out.

With Fat-Cat having easily remembered personalized plates on his Benz, D-Wub had Joe-Joe get his address from a white girl he knew who worked at the BMV. The information was readily given when she learned it came with a $5,000 tip.

Minutes later, Fat-Cat and Jinx sped up to the crib in a Suburban and hopped out clutching extendos. They were walking up to the house when something suddenly dawned on Fat-Cat. Kiona never called him by his street name, which is what was used in the text. It was then he knew it was a set up. But before he could get on defense or warn Jinx, orange flashes of gunfire lit up the night.

Fop! Fop! Fop! Fop! Fop! Fop! Fop!

As Fat-Cat got low and retreated while blindly busting back, Jinx collapsed from a hollow that drove through his hoodie and parked next to his heart.

Emerging from opposite sides of the house, D-Wub went after Fat-Cat as Ghost paused over Jinx to finish him off. "Told you you wouldn't be lucky the next time," he reminded him before he put five in his beard, then ran off to assist D-Wub.

As Fat-Cat was hopping a tall privacy fence, D-Wub stopped, took aim, and let off three shots.

Fop! Fop! Fop!

Shot in the back of his leg, Fat-Cat hollered out in pain as he fell over into a vegetable garden and fumbled the gun. With no time to look for it, he quickly got up and hobbled off.

Fop! Fop! Fop! Fop! Fop! Fop!

Hearing the bullets fly past as the two shooters relentlessly pursued him, Fat-Cat was beginning to doubt that he would ever see Kiona again. Then he came from between two houses and literally ran into a miracle on four wheels, a cop car. Now glad that he had dropped the gun, he threw his hands up in surrender.

The officer driving saw D-Wub and Ghost turn back and run in the opposite direction, then reached for his radio. "I have two armed suspects running northbound on Keltner and Maholland Drive."

After receiving a 911 call of "shots fired" and a possible homicide, T.P.D. had responded to the suburban neighborhood within minutes. The area was currently being swarmed by dozens of patrol cars.

As Joe-Joe witnessed them zip down the block while an overhead helicopter scanned the darkened area for suspects, he knew he had no choice but to put the Durango in drive and pray for D-Wub's safety.

"I'ma stop at a gas station," he said aloud as he pulled away from the curb. "An' if Blood don't call in a hour, we out."

Despite D-Wub and Ghost crawling beneath cars inside someone's garage and lying deathly still, their hidden forms were quickly detected through the helicopters infrared night vision.

Mildly beaten before being handcuffed, they were placed in separate cruisers and taken to the police station where both men's hands and clothes were tested for gunshot residue.

Chapter 25

Two Weeks Later

Rocking orange jumpsuits and matching crocs, D-Wub and Ghost were walking laps around the county's gym as a competitive five-on-five basketball game was underway. Their bonds set at two million apiece, they were both being charged with Jinx's murder.

While Fat-Cat told authorities he couldn't identify either man, their G.S.R. tests had came back positive, and one of the murder weapons had been discovered after a later search. So, even with their team of high-powered attorneys, acquittals would be nearly impossible.

"I been thinkin', Wub," Ghost said as they strolled at a slow pace. "An' ain't no reason for us both to catch a elbow for this shit. So I'ma take out, Blood. All I ask is that you hold me down for as long as you alive." The epitome of a true soldier, Ghost knew D-Wub had more to lose and was willing to dive on a grenade.

A ton of weight suddenly lifted from his shoulders, D-Wub stopped walking and turned to stare Ghost straight in his eyes. "You the realest nigga I ever met, Blood. An' I ain't just sayin' that because of this, but on account of how you been carryin' it since day one. An' my right hand to the Blood Gang, homie, I'ma make sho' you as comfortable as possible while you in here."

Later that night, Ghost was listening to the eleven o'clock news from his cell when he heard something that made him instantly hop up and go out to the dayroom.

"I'm currently standing outside a Central Toledo home where the decomposing body of an eighteen-year-old male, identified as Mukiah Crawford, was found inside a bedroom closet. The body was discovered after a neighbor contacted officials complaining of a foul odor coming from inside the home..."

As Ghost stood there numbly staring at the screen, the cameraman showed police bringing Charlene and Eddie out in handcuffs, while a malnourished Boogie was carried out by a woman from Children Services.

Knowing Moo-Moo had been a member of the Wolf-Pack, other inmates stepped aside and offered Ghost their condolences as he walked back to his cell.

Damn, blood. Why you aint listen to me? Ghost said to himself as he laid down and pulled the cover over his head.

***

Kiona's Lexus coupe was double parked in front of the hospital's E.R. as she rolled Fat-Cat out in a wheelchair. His leg in a cast, the hollow point had broken the tibia in the lower part of his left leg, leaving him on crutches for the next six weeks.

After helping him inside the car, Kiona returned the wheelchair, then slid back in the coupe and drove to the airport in Detroit where she had already booked two first class flights to Atlanta.

With Jinx gone and Shooter facing the needle, Fat-Cat knew it was time to put the city in his rear-view. But before doing so, he had financed Jinx's funeral, which people from all sides attended, dropped a hundred racks on Shooter's lawyer, and left Blueface with a quarter million in pills. While there was nothing more he could currently do for them, he would always be on standby, just from a distance.

As the Boeing ascended into the clouds, Fat-Cat grabbed Kiona's hand and kissed it. "I'll never meet another woman as thorough as you."

Kiona smiled. "I'ma reflection of you, bae."

***

Baby-Herc had been devastated behind the loss of Jinx, who had been like his big brother. But knowing he would want him to continue running toward a successful future, he stayed in college and took his anger out on the football field. He would not let big bro' down.

In Jinx's SRT Dodge Ram, Baby-Herc was leaving a G.N.C. on the outskirts of the city when he saw a familiar face walking down the street. Turning the truck around, he pulled up on him and lowered his window. "What up, Cuzz!?"

"Damn, nigga!" Eli cheesed, "I ain't seen you in a *minute*. Fuck you doin' way out here?"

Baby-Herc held up the G.N.C. bag. "Protein, nigga. You know I gotta feed all these muscles an' shit."

After sharing a laugh, he asked Eli where he was going.

"I'm just 'bout to shoot down to gas station an' grab a Swisher."

Baby-Herc glanced at his watch, then said, "I got class in the mornin', so I can't stay out too late. But come on an' jump in. I'll give you a ride."

He saw Eli considering the invitation with uncertainty and assured him, "Cuzz, you know I ain't on that shit. My focus on goin' to the league. Now hop yo' ugly-ass in the car."

"Aw, I know you ain't talkin'," Eli said and laughed as he walked around to the passenger side. "Wit' yo' big *Shrek* lookin'-ass!"

As soon as his door was closed, Baby-Herc punched the gas and made the Pirelli's scream.

Skrrrtt!

"How you get this?" Eli asked in regards to the supercharged truck. Sitting up on 26-inch Forgis with ostrich seats and an iPad in the dash, he knew Jinx had put a pretty penny into it.

"Jinx gave it to me," he answered as he grabbed a remote that controlled the $10,000 audio system. "Cuzz left me everythang."

The wheels in his mind now rapidly spinning, Eli preyed on Baby-Hercs unselfish nature. "I ain't even gon' lie to you, Cuzz. I'm lightweight doin' bad right now. You think you can let me hold somethin'? You know, just till I get back on my feet?"

"Come on, Eli, you ain't even gotta ask me no shit like that. Just tell me know how much you need."

"Shid," Eli smiled. "Just shoot me like—"

His sentence was cut short as Blueface popped up in the backseat and wrapped a garrote around his neck.

His eyes bulging in fear, Eli violently gagged while desperately grabbing at Blueface's hands, which were gripped tightly around the handles of the tool designed for strangulation.

"I always knew you wasn't built for this shit, nigga," he whispered in Eli's ear as the wire dug into neck, cutting off his oxygen supply. "So it's my pleasure to send yo' weak ass to the other side."

Kweli

Chapter 26

J-Bo's Trial Day

The prosecution side of the courtroom was packed. Settled in the front rows were family members of victims from both crime scenes, and behind them were a legion of uniformed officers who were there to personally witness the conviction of a cop killer.

With the case having gained national attention, there was a slew of camera crews set up around the room. They would capture the defendant's every blink.

A veil of silence fell over the courtroom when the man charged with eight murders and the theft of $3.2 million from a bank's vault was escorted in by four deputy sheriffs. Wearing a charcoal-gray suit over two-tone Stacy's, J-Bo returned their hateful glares with a cool expression.

Wingate had counseled him on the importance of being camera conscious at all times. "Their goal is to paint you as a rabid animal that needs to be put down. So at no point during this trial can you afford to fit that description."

At the defense table, Wingate greeted him with a firm handshake. "How you feelin', champ?"

"Ready to rumble."

As he took a seat, J-Bo turned to acknowledge the small entourage who were attending the trial on his behalf. While on the surface it appeared to be a genuine display, he had never seen either person a day in his life.

From experience, Wingate knew how damaging it could be for a defendant to not have any support present in his section. It suggested to a jury that maybe he was so foul of a person that not even his own family or friends were concerned about his outcome. That could allow their decision to convict on all counts much easier. So, out of allegiance to his client along with his addiction to acquittals, he had made the necessary arrangements.

After persuasive opening statements from both sides, the prosecution began calling its witnesses.

When the woman from the bank, who Ham had sexually assaulted, took the stand and gave a tearful account of the robbery, J-Bo glanced toward the jury box and saw several women dabbing at their eyes. He then looked at Wingate and wondered if he was truly capable of performing miracles.

After hearing testimony from the state's third witness, the judge recessed for the day. "We'll resume tomorrow morning at 9 a.m." he announced before banging his gavel. "This court is adjourned."

As the jury was being led out, J-Bo turned to Wingate. "It might be ugly, Phil."

Knowing he was referring to the jury's emotional state, he shook his head in disagreement. "I wouldn't necessarily say that. What you saw was just a natural reaction to hearin' a sad story. Especially one that involves innocent people."

"Yeah, but–"

"Just relax, baby boy," Wingate cut him off with a wink. "Our turn ain't even came up yet."

Over the next two days, Wingate calmly sat back as the prosecutor hauled in witness after witness. Patience being one of his strong suits, he was waiting for the moment when he would drive a knife into the heart of the state's case.

Not one to half step, when Terry Jones had provided J-Bo with an alibi, he made sure that it was rock solid. A retired college professor named George Steinbecker would testify that on the day of the bank robbery, the defendant had been doing remodeling work on his basement all afternoon. With him being a respectable white man without even a parking ticket on his record, his credibility would be unquestionable.

After the prosecutor firmly established that one of the four assailants involved in the deadly heist had gotten way, he was then ready to put aside the appetizers for the main course.

"Your Honor, the state would now like to call Donald Wharton to the witness stand."

The name not ringing a bell, Wingate scanned the prosecution's witness list, then quickly began flipping through J-Bo's Discovery.

As Wharton lowered his right hand, the judge removed the prosecutor's leash. "You may proceed with your witness, counselor."

"Good afternoon, Mr.—"

"Excuse me, your Honor," Wingate interrupted as he stood up from the table. "But if I could please approach the bench."

The judge looked at the prosecutor, who shrugged in response, then turned back to Wingate. "Is it so urgent that it can't wait until we recess?"

"It is, your Honor."

Telling the stenographer they would briefly go off the record, the judge waved him forward.

In a low but seething tone, Wingate explained that not only was Wharton's name absent from the prosecution's witness list, but also that he had no idea of what he would testify about. "I've never heard of this man until today. So there's no way I could possibly prepare an effective cross exam if the need arose."

With his bushy eyebrows bunched into an irritated frown, the judge signalled for the prosecutor to join the huddle. Then, placing a meaty palm over the mic, he sharply stated, "Mr. Wingate claims he had no prior knowledge of this witness."

The prosecutor scoffed at the statement as if he had already known this was a card the lawyer would play. "Your Honor, I can assure you that I would not stoop so low as to withhold evidence from the defendant's Discovery."

"There's nothing in there pertaining to this witness, your Honor," Wingate said in persistence.

Removing his glasses, the judge closed his eyes while massaging the bridge of his nose. He then called a thirty-minute recess and ordered for the jury to be taken from the room.

"Both of you!" he barked at Wingate and the prosecutor. "In my chambers, *now!*"

Standing behind his massive oak desk with a scowling expression, he glared at both men before addressing the prosecutor. "Can you confirm that you presented the defense with all evidence related to Mr. Wharton?"

"Call Mr. Letner, your Honor, the lawyer initially appointed to the defendant. He'll confirm that I personally handed him a copy of Wharton's report."

"And what exactly would this witness be testifying in regards to?"

His answer left Wingate stunned. It was a blow so crushing to the defense, he knew his client was suddenly in a position from which there was no escape. That was being checkmated in one move.

The judge dialed his bailiff and told her to get in touch with John Letner from the public defender's office.

His phone rung several minutes later, which he put on speaker. "Go ahead, Cindy."

"Sir, I have Mr. Letner on line three."

After bringing him up to speed on the case, the judge asked Mr. Letner if he could recall the prosecutor ever giving him a scientific report from Donald Wharton.

Several suspenseful seconds passed before he answered. "I do, your Honor."

"And I assume this report was enclosed in the defendant's Discovery when you handed it over to Mr. Wingate."

"Absolutely," he lied without hesitation.

Disconnecting the call, the judge pleasingly announced that he would allow the witness to testify. "And Mr. Wingate," he added as they were leaving his chambers, "If you ever again attempt to make a mockery of my courtroom, I'll hold you in contempt."

While Wingate was hardly surprised by the conniving play put down Letner and the prosecutor, he couldn't understand why his client had failed to give him a heads up. As a true chess player, he believed that in most cases, if you studied the board hard enough, there was usually a way out of a jam. But because he had been left in the dark, he was now powerless in preventing his client from being convicted of all forty-seven counts.

J-Bo's observant eyes were locked on Wingate as he walked back to the table without the usual pep in his step. "Wassup, Phil?" he anxiously questioned before he was fully seated.

Wingate gave it to him with no chaser. "They found your D.N.A at the bank."

J-Bo's initial reaction was to shake his head in denial and tell Wingate it wasn't possible. But as his mind raced at an unnatural speed, it took only a split-second to bitterly recall the crucial mistake he had made that day.

Damn, he cursed to himself as he leaned back in his chair and slowly shook his head. *It's over wit'*.

The jury was all ears as forensic scientist Donald Wharton explained how a partially-smoked Black-n-Mild cigar had been found in the bank's parking lot on the day of the robbery. Bagged and tagged as potential evidence, it was rushed to a laboratory for D.N.A. testing, where traces of saliva had been lifted from its tip. It was then entered into a computerized system and compared with all D.N.A. currently on file.

On cue, the prosecutor picked up a small clear bag from the evidence table. "Mr. Wharton, I'm handing you now state's exhibit number 31. If you'll take a moment to look at that. What is state's exhibit 31?

"This is the cigar that was found in the bank's parking lot."

"Is this the same cigar you tested for D.N.A.?"

"It is."

The prosecutor turned to the judge. "Your Honor, the state would move to admit into evidence exhibit 31."

"The state's exhibit will be admitted."

At the defense table, J-Bo was in deep thought as he reflected on the moment when he flicked the Black-n-Mild out the car window. He had thought it was over at that point. How could he have known or even suspected that Juan-Juan would come back and do what he did?

But he knew there was no room for excuses. It all boiled down to his weakness. A weakness that played a role in his mans death and would now be the cause of his own.

With his hands clasped behind his back, the prosecutor casually made his way across the room until he was standing in front of the jury box. Then he swiveled toward Wharton and went in for the kill. "Mr. Wharton, was there enough saliva present on the cigar for purposes of establishing a positive identification?"

"There was."

"Sir, could you please tell the court who the D.N.A. belonged to."

He glanced at the defense table and answered, "Jovante Bowden."

The outbursts inside the courtroom were so explosive, the judge had to yell for order and banged his gavel several times before it quieted down.

"I have just one final question," the prosecutor continued. "When you say the D.N.A. was a positive match, exactly how accurate is that deter`mination?"

"99.9 percent."

The prosecutor turned back to the jury and concluded, "And the defense swore to you in its opening statement that the defendant had *never* been to the city of Columbus, Ohio."

Wearing a smile of triumph as he glided back to his table, he told the judge he had no further questions.

The ball now in Wingate's court, he asked the judge if he could have a moment to speak with his client.

Glancing at the clock, he announced that they would recess for lunch and resume in an hour.

As the courtroom was clearing out, Wingate asked J-Bo what he wanted to do. While there was no recovering from the damage caused by the forensic expert, it was not his life on the line.

J-Bo knew what time it was. But rather than cry, complain, or cower in fear, he would boldly embrace his fate with open arms.

After everyone was back in place inside the courtroom, the judge asked Wingate if he was ready to proceed.

"I am, your Honor," he answered, rising to his feet. As he was on the verge of informing the court of his client's wish to throw in the towel, J-Bo shot out of his chair with lightning speed.

Able to reach the prosecutor before being restrained, he landed two vicious hooks that shattered his nose. Then, further giving the photographers what they wanted, J-Bo fought and screamed like a rabid animal as he was carried from the courtroom.

Kweli

Chapter 27

Four Years Later

Three Brock Lesner-sized guards with crew cuts and stony expressions marched down a dimly-lit tier and stopped in front of cell 22. The senior guard, known as Red-Beard, unlocked the chute and told the inmate inside to cuff up. After he bent down far enough to stick his arms out, handcuffs were clicked over his wrists, then his cell door was popped and shackles were attached to his ankles.

With a guard on either side of him and Red-Beard in the rear, J-Bo shuffled down the tier as other prisoners silently peered from behind the narrow windows of their cells. He was taking a trip that neither man anticipated, but knew would one day arrive—to the death house in Lucasville.

After being sentenced to death by lethal injection, J-Bo had been transferred to Chillicothe Correctional Institution. Called Chilli for short, it was a castle-size prison that housed 3,000 inmates with a separate wing for the condemned. Despite the fact he was now living on borrowed time, he had stepped onto the compound with the mindset that he would stand tall until the end.

So he kept himself well-groomed, exercised daily, and showed no emotion to fellow prisoners or guards. He would not be remembered as someone who crumbled under pressure.

Arriving at Lucasville forty-five minutes later, J-Bo was taken to a segregation unit and placed inside an observation cell made of bars where he would reside until his execution date. Under fluorescent lights that stayed on twenty-four hours a day, his every move would be logged in by a guard seated at a desk directly in front of his cage. While a lot of death row inmates tiptoed on the edges of insanity, and some actually fell over into its bottomless pit, J-Bo was one of the select few who had clung to a clear state-of-mind.

During the years of his incarceration, he had used solitary confinement as an opportunity to reflect over his entire life and learn who he was as a person. And in doing so, he uncovered the real reason behind his present situation. And it was much bigger than leaving the cigar at the crime scene or being ratted out by Ciara.

He had made a life-threatening mistake that people from all over the world could relate to which was being loyal to a fault. That is when you jeopardize your own well-being by being overly loyal to the wrong person or people; the downfall of many.

In J-Bo's case, he had been clearly shown during his federal bid that he and Juan-Juan had grown to become two different people with lives that were meant to go in two separate directions. But because he chose to place what he *thought* was loyalty over his own well-being, he had basically put a gun to his life and robbed it of the chance to ever experience marriage, the joy of being a father, or the feeling of real success.

If only he had understood back then what he now understood about the difficulty in leaving a friend behind. Sometimes the *smartest* decisions be the *hardest* decisions.

***

Ten days later

The death squad showed up at 8:30 p.m. Standing outside J-Bo's cage, the darkly clothed men studied him for the slightest trace of fear. They found it hard to believe that someone so close to death could possess such a calm demeanor. Not only was it uncommon, but for them personally, it was disappointing.

Accompanied by several prison officials, the warden arrived minutes later. "Good evening, Mr. Bowden. Before we began, I was wondering if you'd changed your mind in regards to any of the provisions offered to you?"

Earlier that day, he had refused to meet with the prison's chaplain or partake in a last meal. It was too late for repentance and only animals were fattened up before being slaughtered.

J-Bo eyed the warden with a direct stare and answered, "Let's just get this lil' shit over wit'."

"As you wish," he replied in an icy tone, then began reading the death warrant.

Following J-Bo's convictions, the appeal lawyer assigned to his case had immediately filed an Anders brief. It basically stated that after reading over the entire transcripts, there was nothing to appeal and he wished to be removed from the case. When J-Bo filed nothing in reply, the appellate court granted the lawyer's request and an execution date had been set.

He would not live to see his 26th birthday.

J-Bo was removed from his cell at 11:30 and loaded onto a prison van. They drove through double gates, around the parameter of gun towers and barbed-wire fences, then stopped behind a small windowless building.

Three armed guards stood at the back door as they shuffled up the short path and the group entered what was called The Death House.

In the center of the room was a white-sheeted gurney with wide black straps that hung from its arms, legs, and waist. A floor length curtain was directly behind it, where the medical staff responsible for the injections were hidden. In each corner, there was a different colored phone and up front on a raised platform were two viewing booths for the witnesses. The windows were presently blocked off by long white drapes.

When the shackles were removed from his wrists and ankles, J-Bo climbed onto the gurney with no hesitation. Refusing to give any indication of fear, he had already resolved in his mind that he would starve them of what he knew their racist hearts craved—seeing him weaken in his final moments

Once he was strapped to the gurney with an I.V. inserted into his vein, the blinds to both rooms were drawn aside. Lifting his head, J-Bo first looked toward the viewing booth with the mirrored glass from where he knew the victim's families were watching him. The glare in his eyes was bright and unafraid. If they had came to see a broken man, they had came to the wrong event.

When he turned his attention to the opposite window, he was genuinely surprised by an image he saw standing behind the glass. The uncombed hair had been shaved into a gleaming bald head, and the scraggly beard was now a salt-and-pepper goatee. From appearance, Terry Jones had bounced back.

J-Bo held his stare for a minute, then laid his head back down.

One of the prison officials produced a cordless microphone and approached the gurney to ask J-Bo if he had any last words.

With his face locked into a blank expression, he wordlessly continued to stare at the ceiling, thinking to himself, *In silence I surrender.*

The warden gave a single head nod to one of his assistants, who signalled for the medical staff to begin the injections.

After given a strong sedative, which put him to sleep within seconds, potassium chloride was then fed into his veins. A chemical solution designed to stop the heart, J-Bo would be dead in under two minutes.

A blanket of silence covered the entire building as some eagerly waited for the pronouncement of his death.

Ring! Ring! Ring!

Heads instantly jerked toward the red phone, which they knew was the governor's direct line.

The warden hurried over to answer it. He listened for several seconds before urgently yelling for the medical staff to stop the injection. The governor had personally stayed the execution.

As J-Bo was removed from the gurney and rushed to a hospital, the victims families were outraged, while Terry Jones was overwhelmed with emotion.

His female companion used her thumb to erase his tear tracks. "This is good news, right?"

"Of course it is," he answered after offering a silent prayer of gratitude. "They just spared my son."

Chapter 28

A midnight blue Escalade coasted over the cobble-stone road of a cemetery. The slender brake lights flashed as it came to a stop. Seconds later, Terry Jones exited the passenger side of the truck with two flower bouquets. Expensively clothed in designer sneakers and a leather jacket, he strode across the recently mowed lawn toward Juan-Juan's gravesite.

After learning of Juan-Juan's death, Terry Jones had made arrangements for him to have a decent burial. Because if left up to the state, he knew they would place him inside a pine box and bury it in an unmarked location. And his character would not allow that to happen.

Terry presented Juan-Juan with both bouquets, one from him and the other from J-Bo, then informed him of last night's news. "They spared   J-Bo, youngblood. It was a close call. An' it couldn't of happened without you."

When Juan-Juan had left J-Bo the note asking him to look out for Terry in the event of his demise, J-Bo had given him a half-million from the robbery. He knew it was a lot to give someone who was homeless at the time, but because Juan-Juan considered the man a friend, he treated him accordingly.

With the money, Terry was able to not only pay for Juan-Juan's burial, but also hire Wingate as J-Bo's lawyer. Then when J-Bo lost trial and was sentenced to death, he approached Wingate with another proposal. He would give him $200,000 if he could stop the execution.

Through his political ties, Wingate had been able to personally speak with the governor, who he attended college with, and informed him of J-Bo's traumatic childhood and the need for a sentence commutation. Money being the motive, a deal was made after Wingate offered him a $150,000 in untraceable bills.

With his hands tucked inside his coat pocket as he stared off into the horizon, Terry finally revealed to Juan-Juan one of the burdens he had been shouldering for years. It was the answer to a question Juan-Juan had once asked him as they were seated inside an abandoned house.

"Terry, why you live like this?"

"I can still remember the day I found out J-Bo was my son. I kinda sensed it from the first time I saw 'im, but I had to know for sho'. So I waited till he an' his grandmother left their house one day an' I broke in an' took one of his hats. You know, for hair samples. An' when I got the results back from the D.N.A. test, I cried like a baby, youngblood. 'Cause I knew I had what it took to raise him into a cold-blooded ass man.

But I also knew that I could never face him after what happened that night. 'Cause how could I ever expect love or forgiveness from a boy who witnessed me kill his own mother? So I stayed away, even when I knew how much he needed me. I failed in so many ways, youngblood. Him as a father, an' you as a friend."

Before walking back to the truck, Terry tearfully removed a worn piece of paper from his pocket. "I was goin' through some of my stuff the other day an' came across somethin' you wrote a long time ago. You had balled it up an' threw it in a corner. In hindsight, I know you wanted me to find it. An' because I did nothin' to help you, I'll always feel that you in a place that should've been reserved for me."

He unfolded the piece of paper, then continued, "If you don't mind, youngblood, I'd like to read it."

It was a poem Juan-Juan had written titled, "My Silent Cries".

"The purpose of my life is a mystery to even myself. So if someone hears my silent cries, please reach out an' offer me help.

This has been a difficult life, one that's well beyond my comprehension. I often ask myself, "Why wasn't I smothered in unconditional love an' attention?"

Let me enlighten you as to what happens to a neglected child. Life no longer seems worthwhile, an' rarely will you witness him genuinely smile. I'd like to be a real man, but a real man has never been a part of my life. An' how can you expect me to respect women when my own mother left me to die?

I've grown to become a person without shame. So I admit that while in my mother's womb, I inhaled crack cocaine.

I present myself as tough, but there are many nights when I've actually laid an' cried.

I present myself as tough, but there are many nights when I've actually laid an' cried. 'Cause how is it that I have a heartbeat, but yet feel as if I'm not alive?

I find myself becomin' the same monster as the ones who raised me. But I wish to become somethin'

different, so I ask that someone please attempt to save me.
Don't look at my background an' automatically assume I'm just a hopeless thug. But look deep into my eyes an' you'll realize I'm just someone in desperate need of love."

***

Heavily intoxicated, tears were pouring from Dr. Patterson's eyes as he sat in Olivia's bedroom hugging one of her highschool pictures. He had been at J-Bo's execution last night and couldn't believe the man who he knew was responsible for taking his daughter's life had been spared.

He wondered how anyone could extend mercy toward such a monster. A monster who had deprived him of closure by refusing to reveal the location of her remains.

Draining what was left in the bottle of Jack Daniels, he wiped his mouth with the back of his hand and picked up a loaded .38 special. With the two most important people in his life gone, there was nothing left to continue living for.

Dr. Patterson kissed Olivia's picture before placing the revolver to his temple. "I'm on my way, sweetheart," he said, then squeezed the trigger.

Boom!

***

After his death sentence was commuted to life without parole, J-Bo learned he was being removed from segregation and placed in population. While at first he was not excited about spending the rest of his life inside a kennel, he came to the realization that they might trap him physically, but trapping him mentally was something beyond their control.

"I can make shit happen from right here in this small ass cell," Hh encouraged himself as he laid in his rack. It was then he decided he would write a book and share he and Juan-Juan's story with the world. And by doing so, his life would not be wasted and Juan-Juan's sacrifice would not have been in vain.

As J-Bo was escorted into population, convicts from both tiers began banging on the bars of their cells while hollering out congratulating statements. *"Real niggas don't die! We multiply!"*

Placed in cell 63, J-Bo dropped his mat on the iron slab and looked around at his new kennel.

Yeah, I'ma turn this bitch into a straight office, he thought to himself as he began making his bed.

"Aye, homie," his neighbor called out.

"What's good, bra?" J-Bo answered as he walked to the front of his cell.

"Everybody in this bitch already hip to you, my baby. We been seein' yo' shit in the papers since y'all hit that bank an' shit. So I'm just sayin', if there's anythang you need, don't hesitate to speak on it." He lowered his voice and added, "Weed, squallies, whatever."

"I'm good right now, but I'll definitely keep it in mind."

"An' by the way," his neighbor continued. "I'm Pinewood-T."

J-Bo's eyebrows instantly lifted in surprise. *Ain't no way*, he thought to himself.

"Ain't you from Toledo?" Pinewood-T inquired.

"Fa sho'."

"Yeah, I used to be up there on a regular. I'm from the D, my baby. An' you know we ain't nothin' but like a half hour away."

When Pinewood-T held up a mirror so they could see each other, J-Bo couldn't believe his eyes. This was actually the same man that Ciara had set up for him and Juan-Juan to rob. The same man who he shot in the leg three times.

It's a small-ass world, he thought and smirked to himself as he went back to making up his bed.

Chapter 29

Atlanta

With the tops down, two Lambos and a red Ferrari pulled into a plaza off Bankhead Boulevard and parked side-by-side. In designer clothes and colored diamonds, three savages emerged from the foreigns and swaggered toward a barbershop called Perfection. It was a well-known spot from zone one through six.

When they entered the shop, nearly everyone inside could feel the danger that lurked beneath their mellow expressions. There was no doubt that three killers had just stepped into their presence.

"What's good, potna?" a barber named Earl spoke up, addressing one of the four men.

"We just flew in from OT an' tryna get ready for tonight," he answered with an unblinking stare.

Earl nodded. "A'ight, that's cool. Just grab a token out that box right there an' listen for yo' number."

The seasoned killer pulled out a larger bankroll, counted off $1,000 and pressed it into Earl's mitt. "We don't wait in lines."

Before Earl could respond, the owner came from a back office and locked eyes with one of the three men. Simultaneously reaching toward their waist, they both withdrew semis and leveled them at each other's face.

As workers and customers got low and scurried from the shop, another man came from the back and stood next to the owner two-handedly clutching a 100-round Drako.

"What's craccin, Cuzz!?" Shooter barked as he fearlessly held his weapon in steady hands.

"Shid, what's poppin', Blood?" D-Wub replied, equally unafraid.

After four successful years of marriage and the construction of a multimillion dollar empire, the owner, Fat-Cat, never imagined his past would someday show up on the doorstep of his present.

***

After paying for J-Bo's legal fees and sentence commutation, Terry Jones had migrated to Atlanta where he invested every coin left into real estate. Ambition in his blood, he was now the owner of seventeen properties and two drive-thru convenience stores.

He was locking the door to one of his recently bought houses when a turquoise-colored car pulled up and stopped. Seconds later, an attractive female in her early thirties stepped out.

"Are you Terry Jones?" she asked while walking up.

"I'm afraid not," he lied with a straight face. "But is there a message you would like for me to give 'im?"

Visibly disappointed, she shook her head and replied, "Nah, it's cool. I'll just look somewhere else."

"What you lookin' fo'?" Terry asked as she was turning to leave.

Once a bad bitch, she lowered her head in shame and answered, "Somewhere to live."

For a reason unknown, Terry's heart went out to her. His intuition usually on point, he sensed she was a solid woman who had fallen on hard times.

"What's yo' name?"

"Malikah Howard."

"Nice to meet you, Malikah," he said, extending his hand. "I'm Terry Jones."

Malikah was not all surprised. As a street veteran, she could understand that caution was sometimes necessary.

When he told her she could sign the lease today and pay only the security deposit, she thanked him with an appreciative smile, then went to tell her girl to come back and pick her up in an hour.

Before the car pulled off, Malikah opened its back door and grabbed the hand of a five-year-old boy. His hair in six long cornrolls that touched his shoulders, he wore a serious expression as they walked up.

"Terry, this my son, Booka. Booka, this Terry."

''What's up, Booka?" Terry smiled as he held his fist out for some dap.

The little boy looked away.

"Booka, say hi," Malikah urged him.

He shook his head defiantly. "I'on talk to strangers."

Terry couldn't help but to smirk in approval. The boy was sharp.

Inside the house, Terry was giving Malikah a tour of the upstairs when she asked him where he was from. She could tell he was a foreigner by his lack of a southern accent.

"I'm originally from Ohio. I moved down here a few years ago."

Malikah rubbed a hand over son's head affectionately. "Booka's daddy was from Ohio."

"You say *was*?"He wondered why she spoke on the past tense

"Yeah, he died a few years ago," she promptly explained. "You pro'ly heard about it, it was all over the news."

Goosebumps suddenly appeared on Terry's arms. He looked down at Booka, who he now examined more closely, then asked a question he felt he already knew the answer to. "Who was yo' baby's father?"

Smiling at the memory of him, Malikah answered, "Juan-Juan."

TO BE CONTINUED

**THE COST OF LOYALTY 3
COMING SOON**

Submission Guideline

Submit the first three chapters of your completed manuscript to ldpsubmissions@gmail.com, subject line: Your book's title. The manuscript must be in a .doc file and sent as an attachment. Document should be in Times New Roman, double spaced and in size 12 font. Also, provide your synopsis and full contact information. If sending multiple submissions, they must each be in a separate email.

Have a story but no way to send it electronically? You can still submit to LDP/Ca$h Presents. Send in the first three chapters, written or typed, of your completed manuscript to:

LDP: Submissions Dept
Po Box 870494
Mesquite, Tx 75187

DO NOT send original manuscript. Must be a duplicate.

Provide your synopsis and a cover letter containing your full contact information.

Thanks for considering LDP and Ca$h Presents.

Coming Soon from Lock Down Publications/Ca$h Presents

BOW DOWN TO MY GANGSTA

By **Ca$h**

TORN BETWEEN TWO

By **Coffee**

BLOOD STAINS OF A SHOTTA **III**

By **Jamaica**

STEADY MOBBIN **III**

By **Marcellus Allen**

BLOOD OF A BOSS **V**

By **Askari**

LOYAL TO THE GAME **IV**

LIFE OF SIN II

By **T.J. & Jelissa**

A DOPEBOY'S PRAYER **II**

By **Eddie "Wolf" Lee**

IF LOVING YOU IS WRONG… **III**

LOVE ME EVEN WHEN IT HURTS **II**

By **Jelissa**

TRUE SAVAGE **VII**

By **Chris Green**

BLAST FOR ME **III**

A BRONX TALE III

DUFFLE BAG CARTEL III

By **Ghost**

ADDICTIED TO THE DRAMA **III**

The Cost of Loyalty 2

By **Jamila Mathis**
LIPSTICK KILLAH **III**
Mimi
WHAT BAD BITCHES DO **III**
A HUSTLER'S DECEIT 3
KILL ZONE **II**
By **Aryanna**
THE COST OF LOYALTY **III**
By **Kweli**
SHE FELL IN LOVE WITH A REAL ONE **II**
By **Tamara Butler**
RENEGADE BOYS **III**
By **Meesha**
CORRUPTED BY A GANGSTA **IV**
By **Destiny Skai**
A GANGSTER'S CODE **III**
By **J-Blunt**
KING OF NEW YORK IV
RISE TO POWER III
By **T.J. Edwards**
GORILLAZ IN THE BAY III
De'Kari
THE STREETS ARE CALLING II
Duquie Wilson
KINGPIN KILLAZ III
STREET KINGS 2
Hood Rich

Kweli

STEADY MOBBIN' **III**
Marcellus Allen
SINS OF A HUSTLA II
ASAD
TRIGGADALE II
Elijah R. Freeman
MARRIED TO A BOSS II
By Destiny Skai & Chris Green
KINGS OF THE GAME II
Playa Ray

Available Now
RESTRAINING ORDER **I & II**
By **CA$H & Coffee**
LOVE KNOWS NO BOUNDARIES **I II & III**
By **Coffee**
RAISED AS A GOON I, II, III & IV
BRED BY THE SLUMS I, II, III
BLAST FOR ME I & II
ROTTEN TO THE CORE I III
A BRONX TALE I, II
DUFFEL BAG CARTEL I II
By **Ghost**
LAY IT DOWN **I & II**
LAST OF A DYING BREED
BLOOD STAINS OF A SHOTTA I & II

By **Jamaica**
LOYAL TO THE GAME
LOYAL TO THE GAME II
LOYAL TO THE GAME III
LIFE OF SIN
By **TJ & Jelissa**
BLOODY COMMAS I & II
SKI MASK CARTEL I II & III
KING OF NEW YORK I II,III
RISE TO POWER I II
By **T.J. Edwards**
IF LOVING HIM IS WRONG…I & II
LOVE ME EVEN WHEN IT HURTS
By **Jelissa**
WHEN THE STREETS CLAP BACK I & II III
By **Jibril Williams**
A DISTINGUISHED THUG STOLE MY HEART I II & III
LOVE SHOULDN'T HURT I II III
RENEGADE BOYS I & II
By **Meesha**
A GANGSTER'S CODE I &, II III
By **J-Blunt**
PUSH IT TO THE LIMIT
By **Bre' Hayes**
BLOOD OF A BOSS **I, II, III & IV**
By **Askari**
THE STREETS BLEED MURDER **I, II & III**

THE HEART OF A GANGSTA I II& III

By **Jerry Jackson**

CUM FOR ME

CUM FOR ME 2

CUM FOR ME 3

CUM FOR ME 4

An **LDP Erotica Collaboration**

BRIDE OF A HUSTLA **I II & II**

THE FETTI GIRLS **I, II& III**

CORRUPTED BY A GANGSTA I, II & III

By **Destiny Skai**

WHEN A GOOD GIRL GOES BAD

By **Adrienne**

THE COST OF LOYALTY

By Kweli

A GANGSTER'S REVENGE **I II III & IV**

THE BOSS MAN'S DAUGHTERS

THE BOSS MAN'S DAUGHTERS II

THE BOSSMAN'S DAUGHTERS III

THE BOSSMAN'S DAUGHTERS IV

THE BOSS MAN'S DAUGHTERS **V**

A SAVAGE LOVE **I & II**

BAE BELONGS TO ME

A HUSTLER'S DECEIT I, II, III

WHAT BAD BITCHES DO I, II

By **Aryanna**

A KINGPIN'S AMBITON

A KINGPIN'S AMBITION **II**

I MURDER FOR THE DOUGH

By **Ambitious**

TRUE SAVAGE

TRUE SAVAGE II

TRUE SAVAGE **III**

TRUE SAVAGE **IV**

TRUE SAVAGE **V**

TRUE SAVAGE **VI**

By **Chris Green**

A DOPEBOY'S PRAYER

By **Eddie "Wolf" Lee**

THE KING CARTEL **I, II & III**

By **Frank Gresham**

THESE NIGGAS AIN'T LOYAL **I, II & III**

By **Nikki Tee**

GANGSTA SHYT **I II &III**

By **CATO**

THE ULTIMATE BETRAYAL

By **Phoenix**

BOSS'N UP **I , II & III**

By **Royal Nicole**

I LOVE YOU TO DEATH

By Destiny J

I RIDE FOR MY HITTA

I STILL RIDE FOR MY HITTA

By **Misty Holt**

LOVE & CHASIN' PAPER

By **Qay Crockett**

TO DIE IN VAIN

SINS OF A HUSTLA

By **ASAD**

BROOKLYN HUSTLAZ

By **Boogsy Morina**

BROOKLYN ON LOCK I & II

By **Sonovia**

GANGSTA CITY

By **Teddy Duke**

A DRUG KING AND HIS DIAMOND I & II III

A DOPEMAN'S RICHES

HER MAN, MINE'S TOO I, II

CASH MONEY HO'S

By Nicole Goosby

TRAPHOUSE KING **I II & III**

KINGPIN KILLAZ

STREET KINGS

By **Hood Rich**

LIPSTICK KILLAH **I, II**

CRIME OF PASSION I & II

By **Mimi**

STEADY MOBBN' **I, II**

By **Marcellus Allen**

WHO SHOT YA **I, II**

Renta

GORILLAZ IN THE BAY **I II**

DE'KARI

TRIGGADALE

Elijah R. Freeman

GOD BLESS THE TRAPPERS I, II, III

THESE SCANDALOUS STREETS I, II, III

FEAR MY GANGSTA I, II, III

THESE STREETS DON'T LOVE NOBODY I, II

BURY ME A G I, II, III, IV, V

A GANGSTA'S EMPIRE I, II, III

Tranay Adams

THE STREETS ARE CALLING

Duquie Wilson

MARRIED TO A BOSS...

By Destiny Skai & Chris Green

KINGS OF THE GAME II

Playa Ray

<u>BOOKS BY LDP'S CEO, CA$H</u>

<u>TRUST IN NO MAN</u>

<u>TRUST IN NO MAN 2</u>

<u>TRUST IN NO MAN 3</u>

<u>BONDED BY BLOOD</u>

<u>SHORTY GOT A THUG</u>

<u>THUGS CRY</u>

<u>THUGS CRY 2</u>

<u>THUGS CRY 3</u>

<u>TRUST NO BITCH</u>

<u>TRUST NO BITCH 2</u>

<u>TRUST NO BITCH 3</u>

<u>TIL MY CASKET DROPS</u>

<u>RESTRAINING ORDER</u>

<u>RESTRAINING ORDER 2</u>

<u>IN LOVE WITH A CONVICT</u>

<u>Coming Soon</u>

BONDED BY BLOOD 2

BOW DOWN TO MY GANGSTA

www.ingramcontent.com/pod-product-compliance
Lightning Source LLC
Chambersburg PA
CBHW070011260626
47159CB00005B/1756